Uncle Albert

Uncle Albert

A collection of short stories

Stephen Wade

Priory Press

Published by Priory Press Ltd
The Priory, Abbots Way, Abbotswood,
Ballasalla, Isle of Man IM9 3EQ
www.priory-press.co.uk

First published 2015

ISBN 978 0 9574914 8 9

Edited and typeset by
Frances Hackeson Freelance Publishing Services,
Brinscall, Lancs
Printed in Great Britain by
Bell and Bain Ltd, Glasgow

Contents

Albert's Yorkie Words

Uncle Albert's talk is generally adapted to the reader who might find Yorkshire words and expressions a bit strange. But there are some local words and phrases which might need explanation, so here they are.

Any road   Anyway, nevertheless.

Bairn   A child. A man still playing with a train set would be a 'girt bairn'.

Brass   Money, as in the old adage: 'Where there's muck there's brass.'

Chelp   To answer back, complain, or generally express discontent. This is usually used when someone has been told to do something and mutters to show discontent.

Clout/clout-head   A simple individual, as in 'Tha daft clout-head!'

Feast   The travelling fair (when wagons arrived with their multi-coloured amusements and chaos began; bairns could not be kept at home unless strapped to a chair).

Flicks   The pictures, the movies. Usually, they were either 'bug utches' infested with fleas, or 'back-seaters' where you could take your beloved for a cuddle.

Frame   To get sorted, get organised, usually expressed as 'Frame thysen!'

Gawp   To stare. As a noun, a gawp was a simpleton.

Gert   Great, large, as in 'that gert big spot on yer nose'.

Gurneying   Pulling a daft face, or as Lancashire folk might say, a typical Yorkshire face.

King Cough   This meant whooping cough. You were supposed to catch it by sitting on cold doorsteps or stones.

KOYLI   The King's Own Yorkshire Light Infantry – Albert's alleged regiment.

Lat   A plank of wood, sometimes applied to a person.

Loiner   A person from Leeds.

Lurgy   An illness – anything from measles to flu, or a term to advise a young lass to avoid a certain young chap: 'Stay away, he's got t' lurgy!'

Meanwood   This is an area of Leeds, but in Albert's time there was a mental hospital there. As often happens, such hospitals and asylums tend to be used in common speech to mean that someone is mentally ill.

Midden   A rubbish heap, a mix of all household waste, usually placed by the outside privy, to encourage dangerous bacteria to join in with family life.

Moither   To annoy or pester: 'If these bairns don't stop moitherin' me I'll go barmy!'

Mun   Must. 'Tha mun get aht o' road' – You must move out of my way.

Neb a beak, or a nose, as in, 'Get tha neb aht o my business!'

Night-closet This is the polite word for the store of human defecation by the midden, gathered in the outside privy. There are several degrees of refinement, or lack of it, in this group of words, ranging from 'number two' or 'pooh' right across the spectrum to 'shite'.

Nowt Nothing: 'It were summat and nowt' – It was of no importance.

Owt Anything: 'I can't tell thee owt'.

Pinny An apron: standard uniform for Bessie.

Old sweat An old soldier, a veteran of the wars.

Rooky Rhubarb.

Rum Odd or strange: 'It were a rum do' – said of something that is hard to understand or to explain.

Scutters An expressive word meaning diarrhoea (easier to spell of course).

Sithee 'You see' as in, 'I backed three winners sithee … ' Can also be used simply to grab the attention: 'Sithee … '

Tanner six old pence – or, in modern cash, two and a half pence.

Tha/thee/thy The old Saxon second person, used before we had 'you' and 'yours'. So, we have 'Tha's late and I've told thee afore, get thy skates on'

Tick Credit. 'I'd like to buy it on tick, mate.'

Tiddler A small silvery fish, no bigger than your average nail. But also used of a weedy, small bairn.

Tyke A Yorkshire person. This can be used as a term of abuse, even within Yorkshire. So, fans of Huddersfield Town call fans of Barnsley, and the club, Tykes. 'You little Tyke' means 'You little rogue'.

Utching up   To utch up is to move along, on a seat, to make room. Often you were asked to utch up on the back seats of the pictures.

Wassock   A term of abuse applied to someone who irritated you.

Introducing Uncle Albert

HOW CAN I START TO DESCRIBE my Uncle Albert? Well, we'll start with him as the Poet Laureate of complainers. Just as some men take up marquetry or assembling plastic kits, he took up chelp. He had a room for it at home, custom-built. His moaning was usually related to his illnesses. When his piles were throbbing the front room was turned into a torture chamber. His daughter-in-law used to pretend to hoover the shed just to keep out of his way. Complaining were a vocation to him. The rumour was that he practised in front of a mirror, screwing up his nose, frowning and saying 'Typical bloody government' in different voices. He said it one way for the bus queue, one way for the bookies, and in a specially irritating way for the saloon bar.

He's difficult to explain because he was a one-off. These days, you might meet a semblance of him in a local museum or on one of these dressing-up heritage days when ancient outfits are dug out of charity shops and some daft bloke walks around like someone out of *Dad's Army*. Well, he wasn't like that –

he was himself, and he came out in his tales. In another age, he would have been some kind of rambling raconteur. Folk would have bought him drinks all night, just to keep his stories flowing.

He was a plain and simple man, with few pleasures and passions, but these he took seriously, working hard and playing hard. He could have been taken for a living stereotype of the Tyke, with his flat cap, waistcoat and fob-watch, and his love of beer and cricket, but there were so many things about him that made him unique, that a generalization would be wrong.

Of course, his speciality was food. He deeply resented any food put in front of him that wasn't flesh. His daughter-in-law tried to pass off a nut cutlet as a bit of tongue once. Within half a minute she was in the shed again. He had problems with eating: he only had half a stomach but he could fart like an elephant. It was a mystery why. This had another side-effect. He used to get a bad attack of the scutters if he ate too much rich food. He had to work hard to hold it in. He developed a walk with bum-cheeks closed, clamped tight like. When he passed certain parts of Leeds he got cat-calls.

I should also mention Albert's religious persuasion. He was the only member of the Plymouth Brethren to live in West Yorkshire. Of course, every place in the county thinks it's the best, and he was the same – he loved Gawpham and wouldn't have lived anywhere else. Folk in Huddersfield say Batley folk eat their first-born, I'm told. Such is the fierce Yorkshire affection for the home town and the contempt expressed about anywhere else, though it's said with humour.

But he had beliefs, of some kind. He saw God as a sort of headmaster and that folk had to try to be prefects and win house points. The problem was, the Devil kept hitting you and he had a gang. God's gang were always somewhere else when you needed them, he said, supping tea and eating muffins by a log fire.

He had bad eyesight. Folk thought he'd been down t' pit in the war – a reserved occupation. Truth is, he'd ruined his eyes studying form wearing his mother's glasses. The racehorses were his obsession. He said he had systems. Like, maybe a hoss would wink at him in the paddock. Or sometimes he'd back the one that evacuated itself before the race. 'That'll beat the handicapper!' he used to shout.

Of course, Albert was a quarter Scotch, or so he said. His dad, Tommy Argyle, wandered from Glasgow and found a lass in Leeds. She weren't lost, she had just forgotten to go home. But Tommy Argyle might have been a myth. One of the features of Uncle Albert's life is that it slipped between reality and legend every day. Somewhere in the middle of that mess of living life to the full, there was an honest Yorkie bloke making an honest penny – as well as trying to do the bookies out of a few pounds.

There was Scottish blood in his veins any road: IOU negative. Though it went positive when he was asked to get a round in.

No, seriously, he got stirrings in his loins when he heard a Rabbie Burns song. His Y-fronts were tight. They'd worn thin, being made in Chile.

Like all Scotsmen, Albert liked a flutter. He used to bet each-way in a three-horse race and hope nobody would notice. He did all these superstitious bets. He'd back four hosses all called Bob because his Uncle Bob had rung the night before – things like that. They would all lose, then in the results on the radio, you'd hear one called Bold Robert had won at 33–1.

He once took the Argyles seriously. He was descended from that clan, he said. So he took out all these books, mugged

3

up on kilts and plaids, learned some words, all that. He even listened to Andy Stewart records. Alice, his daughter-in-law, spent hours hoovering the shed in that period, I recall. Then he packed it all in because Scotland was too far from Wetherby racecourse. But he did put a coat of arms on the wall. I think he got ripped off, as he bought it at Wakefield market and it had two naked women clutching a suggestive-looking dirk. The plaid was pink and yellow as well.

He backed all the horses whose names began with Mac-something. This went on for a month or so. More Fitz- and O'- names came in, so he looked for any possibility of Irish ancestry instead. He was always easily swayed, and that led him into bother, but everybody said he had a heart of gold, and they were not far wrong. He was one of a dying breed.

They usually potter about Yorkshire villages, these old blokes, offering advice to all and sundry, lamenting that the world has gone to the dogs, and offering rosy-coloured nostalgia to any fool who might stop and listen. But Uncle Albert had another dimension to him. He was a sensitive soul hidden under a thick winter coat and a hairy face. He was a bundle of stories, and this collection is a selection of his best adventures. In his earlier days, he had his wife, Bessie, to restrain him a bit, but as a widower let loose among steady drinkers and romancers, he flourished; although we only have to look at the story of him losing her, in the following pages, to see the depths of his emotion in that respect. As I've said, he worked hard and he played hard.

Finally, at heart, Uncle Albert was a poet. Few people around Gawpham knew exactly what kind of poet he was, because he kept his best rhymes for special occasions, and he was at his best on the theme of death. His elegies and eulogies could have rivalled Wordsworth, some said. He liked to recite his little poems like this one, sometimes, when in a sentimental mood. He called it 'Epitaph for the Last Tram in Leeds'

> Rattling red monster astride the lines,
> Running through my youth
> With other joys like Woodbines;
> Noisy, gauche, alien, uncouth,
> You emerged from yellow city smog
> Crackling in like fate.
> Shame about Mrs. Mason's dog,
> Who crossed the line quite late.

The following tales will hopefully give readers a glimpse or two of this remarkable Tyke, Yorkshire's finest, and a representative of a breed of northerner now quite rare to find in the White Rose county.

Uncle Albert and the
Midden Ghost

THE WHOLE VILLAGE OF GAWPHAM knew Uncle Albert's opinion of old Mrs Barber. This was the lady who, widowed many years before, had lost her husband Arthur in the struggle with Hitler, and since then she had lived on scraps and odd jobs, doing anything anywhere for folk around the village. But that was not all: she was rumoured to have the gift of second sight. This frightened off a few folk, but the less sensitive were not bothered, and would stop and have a chat with her without fear of being cursed or told that they were being followed by the Grim Reaper.

It was this special attribute that caused Uncle Albert to be seen in the street accosting her and sometimes teasing her about her claim to have conversations with those who had passed on. He was bold enough to rib her a bit, but he never went too far, as he still believed in keeping his options open when it came to the presence of the next world in this one.

This troubled relationship came to a head one day when Mrs Barber, shawled and swathed in her layers of clothes, with a felt hat pulled down over her yellowy face, walked slowly up Low Fold dragging her little wooden barrow behind her, shouting, 'Firewood! Penny a bag … Firewood!'

Albert, on his way out rabbiting with Timmy his golden Labrador, stopped and stared at her.

'Sarah Barber … how such as you could go pinching bits of wood and then have the cheek to sell it back to folk … well, that's beyond me. And you a respectable woman, as was, before your Arthur copped a bullet.'

Mrs Barber pulled herself up to her full height of five feet four, dropped the handle of her barrow, and pushed up the neb of her hat before responding. 'Albert Peddle, there's a demon after you, and he'll come at dark. You think on, old lad!'

'You're nobbut a witch, Sarah Barber. Years back they would have burned you!'

'Well at least I do honest work. I never pinched this wood, and tha knaws it!'

A little crowd had now gathered, including the shoeless and ragged Slack family, all five of them below the age of twelve and out for mischief, and simple Nellie Noblock who moithered everybody to death just by being herself.

A chorus of high-pitched voices condemned Uncle Albert with cries of 'Shame on you!' and of 'Picking on a woman!' It was more than he could stand, and he muttered a curse or two and took himself off to the Tanhouse fields to murder some rabbits for tea.

Now, back in the fifties when this was happening, in parts of Yorkshire such as Gawpham, not only was toilet paper a thing of the future, but so were actual toilets. The usual place where the villager could go to attend to the call of nature was the outside privy, and that was the case here. There were two privies, side by side, each with its little wooden lat of wood with a neat hole for the Gawpham bottoms to squat over, and gradually, as time went on, and before the night-closet men came to clear out the human waste, a most offensive smell developed. Going to the privy was consequently something of an ordeal, and some folk would put off their visit for as long as possible, until legs were crossed and bottoms were clasped to such a point that nature won the day, and the privy was visited, come what may.

That same night, when the autumn chill was settling in and making folk reach for extra blankets, Uncle Albert, wearing the clothes he wore every day – well-rubbed and shiny dark blue suit and waistcoat with fob-watch, flat cap and mud-caked brown boots, felt the need to visit the said privy.

The Slacks knew that this was likely, as it was a habit with Albert to walk right around the back of his cottage and past the Slack's house to get to the privy, which was situated next to the midden, the brick building where refuse and muck was thrown, mixed with ash from the coal-fires. The little Slacks had heard about the demon, and they were determined to create one.

Uncle Albert was seen walking, or rather rolling, as that was his usual gait, around the back of the houses, with a bundle of bits of torn newspaper in his hand. This was the usual source of toilet paper in those days, and folk had been know to run out to the privy to find the racing results when some unsporty family member had torn up the local paper for use on the family bottoms.

As he entered the privy and shut the door, the smallest and most agile Slack, little Freddie, squatted behind the building and, on a signal from the other Slacks, who were watching and listening, waiting for Albert to be sitting and busy evacuating, he let out a wail that would have made the strongest Yorkie labourer get up and run for safety.

Albert, about to use the first square of *The Daily Sketch* on his behind, jumped up when he heard the wail, thinking that the demon prophesied by old Mrs Barber had arrived to torment him. As he sprang out of the privy, pulling up his trousers and throwing the newspaper out onto the grass, all the little Slacks gathered to stand in a line outside their house and snigger at him. He soon understood that the little ragged-arsed rabble had been responsible for the bother.

Albert was not a man to be crossed, and after gathering himself and then seeing that it was all a prank, soon got to them and grabbed the biggest, scrawny Nellie Slack, by the ear, and set about telling her off.

But in between his rants and threats of telling her mother and fetching the constable, there was a lull. For only a few seconds there was quiet – at least from the kids – but not from the midden. Albert and the Slacks froze, stopped all movement, and turned their gaze to the solid brick rectangle of the midden. There was now a shrieking from that heap of garbage, and it was like a voice tormented in Hell.

The Slacks were back in their house in seconds, and Uncle Albert, not wanting to appear unmanly, was deciding whether or not to go and investigate. Every inch of his courage was gathered up as he took a few steps towards the midden, expecting some horrible tormented soul to emerge and scuttle across in front of him. He went closer and closer, and there was still an unearthly moaning from somewhere in the darkness; then he froze stiff, subdued every little sound his movement or clothes could make, and fixed his stare on the mound of refuse and ash. After a minute or so, something moved in the oozing, soupy mass of detritus, and the stink was so strong that it was like a wall of rotten eggs blocking his way.

At that instant, he realised that he had left something in the privy, something valuable and special to him – his scarf. It was not any old scarf, no, it was his Forley Rangers WMC football team scarf, and he treasured it. Forgetting all danger from whatever it was that was frightening him, Uncle Albert ran to the privy, yanked the door open and looked in, expecting to see his scarf. But there was nothing there at all except the shreds of scattered newspaper.

He had had enough. Albert turned and ran, quick as he could, round past the Slack's house and home. When his son and daughter-in-law, Derek and Alice, asked what was wrong, he couldn't give an answer, and tried to pretend nothing was wrong. That night, he found it hard to sleep, even after three pints of Tetley's bitter.

Then the next day, as Albert was walking down to the club for a game of darts, there was Mrs Barber, pushing her barrow of firewood. He didn't want to speak to her, so he put his chin towards the stone cobbles and tried to walk briskly past. But she looked up, unbending her old, arched frame, and asked him, 'You lost something, Albert Peddle?'

He stopped and frowned. 'Might have done, might have done!'

'Here you are … brought to me at midnight, by your demon. It's looking out for you, but only if you're good to it! It won't leave you, old lad. Never.'

Uncle Albert Goes Carol Singing

ALBERT SHOULD NEVER HAVE GONE WITH THEM. I mean, he'd just sat down to play battleships with his brother Willis, who was half-blind and very slow, so he would have won the treacle toffees easily, but then Roy, his nephew, said that carol singing would earn a few quid, and Albert had lost a lot on the hosses that week. But then Roy always brought trouble, so he should have known. They said he was born with a caul over his face and that this was lucky – but only for Roy, everybody reckoned.

So there they all were five minutes later, Uncle Albert in charge, lining up by the door, wrapped up in big scarves, some of the older ones tipsy. Aunty Pat tried to kiss everyone and the kids who didn't duck in time got big smackers on their foreheads.

Albert gave advice as usual: 'Now, allus sing proper. None o' this devious stuff like "We've been singing, honest." We give value for their brass, right?'

'Course not, what do you think we are, Uncle Albert?'

11

'Little beggars ... but if you're good, we can get chips!'

They trudged out into the Christmas night, which seemed like a stage waiting for a performance: still and silent as a midnight lane, with a dark blue cast over everything. It was bitterly cold. They felt drips on their nose-ends and their fingers stung with the chill, even under their gloves.

There was a mumbled complaint from Sidney, who was virtually a midget and who wore three pieces of cardboard in his shoes to lift him half an inch. Then there was the humming, tuneless rendition of *Little Donkey* from Christine who knew just the first few words of every carol you could mention. Roy was six feet tall and painfully thin. Uncle Albert said he shouldn't walk over grates or he would slip in and be eaten by rats. Uncle Willis said that he would have no bother there as Roy would eat the rats first.

Then there was Mike at the back, who could sing Methodist hymns but since his mam had died he had wandered from all belief, and his dad was the subject of family scandal because he drank beer at home and swore if Hunslet RLFC were losing on a Saturday afternoon.

It began well though. Christine had been given the toffee tin to hold out ready for the small change, and Sidney had been told to practise his dumb face. 'They should take pity on that', Uncle Albert said. He was in command and would do the talking, and Roy had to stay back and whine a bit.

The first house we came to was an end-house on Balaclava Street. It had a posh new gate, so they were hopeful there. They crept up the drive and took their positions. Albert whispered the orders and then Roy knocked loud enough to wake the dead. Someone started singing 'Good King Wenceslas' and Christine hummed something else; Sidney sang an Elvis song, and in the midst of all that the door opened and a grizzled head popped out and snapped, 'Yes?'

Roy said the formula: 'We've been singing, like.'

'Like what?' The man at the door asked.

Uncle Albert, being the leader, said, 'Carols.'

'Oh have you?' The man was surly now.

'Yes, honest,' said Roy, 'and my brother Sidney – he's slow-witted!'

The man looked challenging. 'Well, I didn't hear you!'

At that point, Uncle Albert decided to brazen it out, look at the ground and then look up as if appealing to Heaven, and hope that the man felt some pity. Sidney had no control of his face, and his expression was so grotesque that Albert had him marked down as a future gurneying champion.

'Oh here you are then … Happy Christmas!' The man said, dropping a coin into the toffee-tin.

'Oh this is the stuff … stroll on, easy brass!' said Uncle Albert, and they moved on, repeating the process four or five times. We even made Sidney emphasise his movements a bit but he looked like the Hunchback of Notre Dame so we gave up and left it to nature.

There was a slight hiccup at old Ma Barber's as she was bow-legged and it took her ages to get to the door. Somebody said, 'She couldn't stop a pig in a passage!' and they all giggled. In fact, they had to sing the same line six times before she came, and as she opened the door, Roy sang something from Doris Day and she gave him a look that said he was like something stuck to the sole of her shoe. She was a queer sort. Folk said she used to suck the chocolate off chocolate brazils before she gave them away as a present.

'Well sing us another and you can have a tanner!' she said, almost smiling.

'Ha ha … are you willin' for a shillin?' Roy sang, wiggling his backside. Uncle Albert tutted and told him to behave.

It was sheer greed that led them to disaster. They shivered at the end of Inkerman Street, and Albert counted out a pound and ten bob, and mumbled about going home. But Roy's thoughts were on more ambitious things. 'Look up there Uncle', he said, pointing to a grey and white house standing on its own by Caddiman's Farm. It was the Chesneys' place. They were loaded with money and would surely pay well.

'Just one more call, eh?' Roy asked.

They all agreed and trudged up the slippery, cobbled hill. Some of them had cut their knees on that road before, and they associated it with a dark star. They were right, as it turned out.

Albert knocked on the door. As the adult in charge, he directed everyone to sing a few lines of 'We Wish You a Merry Christmas', and then a shining, happy face greeted them from the yellow-lit doorway. There were festivities going on behind in the sitting-room. Clearly, it was party time at the Chesneys' and someone was at the piano, playing something classical.

'Exquisite! Do come in and sing for us! We love a choir.' This was said by a chubby lad, wearing pink, who chuckled all the time.

Albert tried to explain about not being a choir, but a well-dressed lady smelling of perfume chivvied them into the room and lined them up behind a long sofa. There was plaster above them, moulded into forms of flowers, and chubby little angels with bows; there was a roaring wood-fire, a table piled with food, and a ring of red faces gathering into an audience. They settled comfortably on cushions and chairs as the choir shuffled into line, each trying to hide behind someone else until they were in a frightened huddle.

'Now everyone, the Gawpham town choir has dropped in to give us some festive cheer', the posh woman said to all and sundry. There was massive applause, and there were about thirty people ready to be entertained. Roy ordered that they should line up in a straight line, and Sidney did his best daft face, hoping that would distract the audience from noticing his incompetence.

Uncle Albert, being in charge, decided that he would sing his favourite song at the top of his voice, to cover all their inadequacies, so the audience were treated to 'In the Bleak Midwinter' in broad, deep Yorkie tones, accompanied by jerks and spasms from little Sidney.

Everything seemed to be doing very well, until Albert noticed Sidney's face. It had that red, concentrated expression you see when a baby is about to create something in a nappy. Then, there was the evidence: a growing puddle on the rich, deep blue carpet beneath them.

But the crowd was oblivious to all that. When the choir finished, folk came and plopped coins and folded notes into Christine's tin box and they were given mince pies and sweets, before being ushered out with smiles and farewells.

'There'll be a stain there!', complained Albert on the way home.

'That lot – they'll think it were wine any road!' Sidney said.

They were all so excited by the money and the food, and by the thought that the police might be sent for, that they didn't realise until they got home that they had the wonderful sum of eight pounds in the tin and a scribbled note reading 'See you all next year' in it.

Albert thought he never should have gone. He should have stayed at home and played battleships, but Roy wasn't worried. 'Let's go again – but in disguise', he said brazenly. Still, a

15

little voice in Albert's head troubled him, as he imagined someone finding the stain. Later that night, he crept back to the Chesney's house and put a bottle of stain remover on the doorstep.

But every Christmas after that, Uncle Albert cracked his joke as the family assembled: 'I think we should sing "By the Rivers of Babylon We Sat Down and Wept" when we get to the Chesney place, eh?'

Uncle Albert and the Lost Ring

IN GAWPHAM BACK IN UNCLE ALBERT'S DAY, doctors and barbers were too expensive to consider unless there was an extreme emergency. For that reason, folk managed with self-help arrangements and used what talent they had. If a woman could look a would-be bride up and down and then cut out a pattern for her bridal gown, then that was fine. If a man had a certain level of skill with a spade then who on earth would need to employ a gardener?

This line of thought was carried into extreme cases, as in the strange tale of young Harold Beck who had a crick in his neck. This was first noticed at school when he watched a game of table-tennis. The teacher noticed that the game was accompanied by a *click click*, coming from Harold, every time the ball was knocked over the net.

His mother said that he did it at home but that it didn't stop him from playing soldiers or from climbing trees, and anyway, medicine was frightening to him. The rule was: *if there's summat up, get it straightened yourself.* This led to folk walking around stinking horribly because they had a mushroom poultice on their chest, or kids with lumps of wood in their shoes to sort out flat feet, which the school worried about for some reason. As for toothache, well, remedies abounded, including Uncle Albert's standard mucky mixture, which was a muddy brew of herbs, whisky and bits of animal extracts designed to murder all bacteria by the established method of making the victim spew his or her guts out. Impressionable locals limped about the streets, appealing to people's pitiful responses lamenting the fact that poor Norman has the African Flu or little Lizzie has an incurable tic.

Uncle Albert was always one to take advantage of any opening for his talents, and he was famous for his skill with blades of all kinds. He had a belt of knives, like a professional chef, and took pleasure in skinning the beasts he caught when out hunting with Timmy. One flash of his jacket, revealing these fearsome implements, and the toughest ruffian would flee in terror. But he was also handy with scissors.

This confidence led to his establishment of a barbering service, and the only problem was where to set up his chair and throw a cloth over his clients before lopping off their fringes and tufts. He eyed the village shop at one time, but the back room was cluttered with tins, boxes and three old dogs in baskets. Then he studied the club, and suggested to the committee that a part of the snooker room could be used, but he was told to go away and get a bank loan.

Now, to a man with an irregular income, derived from selling dead animals down the Mason's Arms, and clumps of rhubarb outside the church on Sundays, a bank loan was out of the question. He believed only in dirty money anyway, and had his own bank in a wooden box on the far, light-deprived shelf of his hen-house in his allotment. Once a week, he crept into the shed, breathing in feathers and hen-droppings as he disturbed the creatures in their dark den, and he opened his little box and counted out his pound notes, ten-bob notes and any IOUs he had from debtors who still hadn't paid him for their apples, radishes or mushrooms. He had even been known to barter bunches of mint in exchange for a sausage, so inventive was his skill in survival. Some said he lived on the proceeds of his daughter-in-law's cooking and gardening, and on his pigs, and how he could afford four pints of beer every night in the club was one of the modern Wonders of the World.

With this in mind, his determination to cut locks eventually paid off. The answer was to use the garden. Albert lived in one half of Low Fold cottage, and his son and daughter-in-law, Derek and Alice, in the other half. Since Albert's wife died in the war (brought on by bombing raids they said) Albert had fended for himself and worked to acquire funds or do favours from and in all quarters.

One Friday afternoon in summer it began. He set up his high chair in the middle of the plot, surrounded by rhubarb and raspberry bushes, and invited all the village parents to send their offspring, hairs to be cut at thruppence a go.

Now, the centre of Alice's garden was noted by local courting couples for its privacy. There was a line of apple trees down one side of the acre it covered, and a square of shrubs in the heart of the garden, surrounding the fruit bushes. This left a cosy little patch left for growing lettuce, and the young lovers would sneak into it at dusk, unobserved, for their trysts. On the night before the scheduled hair-cutting session, young Roy, accident-prone and clumsy, and now at the age of fourteen, took his beloved there to express his feelings for her.

Roy had seen too many B movies and saw that glittering rings tended to attract young ladies, and that a marriage proposal was a good idea if you were to experience the joy of being kissed. At least, he thought it would be a joy, but so far in life, kissed only by aunties and parents, he was not sure if joy was the right word for the sensation.

Roy, squatting next to his girl, had a ring in his pocket, bought at the last travelling feast for tuppence; it was a lovely shiny silvery colour and had two tiny red glass balls in it that could have been rubies if you had enough imagination. He brought it out and held it out to his girl, whose name was Ivy, in his closed fist. But it was growing very dark, and as he did that, something ran across his foot, and clearly it ran across his girl's foot. Because she sprang to her feet and screamed, 'Rat! A rat!' Being gallant, Roy also jumped up to help, and the ring fell from his grasp.

There followed a desperate search for the ring. 'It were for you … I was going to propose we get wed!' he said, down on his hands and knees. Ivy was both shocked and scared.

'What? Wed me? You can't do that.' She sounded alarmed and disgusted, so he sat up in the middle of the raspberry bushes and asked what the problem was.

'I'm going to marry Eddie Cochrane, that's why!'

'Who's he? Where does he live?'

'Oh you don't know owt … I'm off home for some supper!' Ivy left him in the dark, his ring lost, and his feelings bruised.

The next afternoon, by four o'clock, Uncle Albert's chair was in place. He was dressed for the part, wearing a khaki coat over his mucky blue suit, and with combs and scissors in the top pocket. He even made a barber's pole out of old football socks (his team Forley Rangers having a red and white strip), wrapping the socks around a brush handle and sticking it among the rhubarb leaves.

The children lined up, giggling and joking, seeing this as a big adventure, and some parents had come as well, out of curiosity. 'Now little bairns first … ' Albert said, bending down to pick up his baking bowl.

On seeing this, one mother called out, 'Hey, what's that?'

'My equipment … my bowl.'

'For what, tha daft clout?'

'Mrs Slack, I use it to cut the hair … short back and sides, all snipped around the bowl.'

Mrs Slack was not happy. 'What? They look like bloody monks!'

'Well, do you want to pay sixpence or tuppence missis?' Albert asked.

'Oh all right then. But if they get laughed at in school I shall come looking for thee!'

Uncle Albert snipped away, cutting around the bowl, and then using his razor around the back and sides, and boy followed boy. The clumps of fallen hair built up and up into great heaps of shorn locks, and by six o'clock the customers were all done, all walking away like little Friar Tucks, and in Albert's pocket the coins jangled and he smiled in anticipation of some well-earned beer.

As for Roy, he was not too bothered about being rejected by Ivy. No, after all, Ivy had a sister called Clara and she was just as brimming with charm and allure as her sister. Consequently, he needed that ring. Roy loitered around the garden, and seeing that Uncle Albert was finished, he used that part of his brain that tended to function when there was a vested interest, and offered to clean up the piles of hair, to keep Alice happy. After all, she wouldn't want rolls of kids' hair clogging up her fruit bushes.

'That's right good of you lad … go ahead. It's worth a tanner', Uncle Albert said, as he jingled his coins again and headed for the club.

Young Roy had the common sense to borrow a brush and a shovel, along with an old tea-chest that Alice had in the shed, and he was soon labouring away, filling the chest with hair. Alice watched him and kept giving him encouragement and compliments, along with a promise of a bowl of raspberries, and he soldiered on, finally having the patch cleared before it was too dark to carry on.

Roy's problem then was to find the ring. It had to be in that garden somewhere. He hadn't seen it in the curly locks of hair he had been collecting, so somewhere in that few square yards of muck there was the ring. He asked to borrow a torch and said he would be looking for the last bits of hair, as Alice brought him the torch and went inside. At last he was alone, and with the torch, surely he could find that ring.

As the world of Gawpham settled down for the night in front of frothy pints or dresses needing hems to be stitched, young Roy searched under every leaf and every little stone or pebble, but to no avail. He went off home, down-hearted, and racked his brain about where the ring might be.

The next morning, Alice went out to check the tea-chest, and saw that the best thing to do was to take all the hair and burn it, out in the metal incinerator. Uncle Albert was up and about, in the allotment to feed and check the pigs, with his braces dangling down over his dark blue trousers, and as he rubbed his face with his pudgy hands, farm-yard muck was lodged in his grey moustache and in his scruffy very slight excuse for a beard. He saw Alice with the tea-chest and went to help. As luck would have it, in the first clump of hair he grabbed, he saw the shiny ring. 'My God!' he said, staring first at the ring and then at Alice, 'I don't believe it ... this is our Bessie's ring. I mean, her engagement ring. Well I'll go to the end of Morley and smack me lips! Would you credit that? She lost this ring back before the war, and she cried about it for days! Do you believe in miracles, our Alice?'

But as Uncle Albert held it up to look at it, Roy arrived, as he had realised that morning that his ring, nowhere in the soil, must be in the box of hair.

'Oh, Uncle Albert ... you found my ring!'

'Found your ring? You're talking out of your backside lad ... this is my Bessie's ring. These mun be rubies, see!'

'No Uncle Albert, they're not rubies. I bought that ring at the feast last May. Sorry to say that like.'

At that point, Alice, with a woman's wisdom and common sense, directed Albert to bite it, to see if it was rubies or glass. 'Are you sure that's what you do, Alice?' Albert was doubtful. But she nodded and smiled and so he went ahead and clamped his front chompers on the stones. There was a crack and a yelp of pain from Albert.

'I think he's broken a tooth!' Roy said, his tone accusing Alice of being at fault, with her bad advice.

'Sorry Dad ... maybe I was wrong ... here ... ', she found a handkerchief and gave it to him, 'this should mop up the blood.'

'My bloody tooth!' Albert wailed.

'Never mind Uncle Albert,' Roy said, trying to sound optimistic, 'You know that Mr Bateson at number eleven? Well, he's bought a white smock and some pliers, and he's going in for some dentist work.'

'Not Bateson? He's got hands as steady as a sewing machine needle!' Albert said.

'Well, he's serious about it, my Mam says. He's saving up for a drill!' Roy didn't realise that his words supplied an element of torment to poor Albert, who was still in doubt as to whether or not the ring was the one he had given to Bessie all that time ago.

Uncle Albert Escapes Sudden Death

UNCLE ALBERT WAS ALWAYS SAYING things to make you laugh, and he had a store of little gobbets of humour that allowed him to show off and crease his face with one of his unforgettable smiles. One of his favourites was when he would roll up his shirt-sleeves and raise one fist, saying, 'Which do you want? This one is Leeds Infirmary … ' Then he would raise the other one and add, 'And this one is sudden death.' But there was one time when he was very close to sudden death, and he was never sure whether to laugh or pray and give thanks to the Almighty when he spoke of it.

It was all because of the Feast that came twice a year to the village. On this occasion, Albert's old friend Norrie Hissop, the local historian, had opened up debate about the origin of the village's name. The hairy and full-bellied Norrie was propounding at a table in the club opposite Uncle Albert (who was in his own seat, which nobody else could sit on).

'Now tha knows as well as me, Gawpham comes from the Anglo-Saxon for *little settlement by the river Gaw*. When the Feast gets set up, we shall have a pageant and a parade – and the brass band – starting off with a talk by my good self on the river and the early people. It's no use arguing, Albert, I'm a published historian.'

'Phaw! Published in the local rag, the *Gawpham and Kittleworth Clarion*. Tha calls that published, Norrie Hissop?'

'Better than thee any road, Albert Peddle!' Norrie took a long pull of his pint.

'Well tha's wrong! Gawp, meaning *slow-witted bloke who stares* ... and ham, meaning pig-meat. It's the place where the gawps made pig-meat! Problem solved!'

The discussion plodded on, nobody prepared to give in, and Norrie Hissop carried on his research, while Uncle Albert planned the pageant and the band. When he was young, back in the Great War, he said, everybody had pageants and parades. From his corner seat in the Gawpham Working Men's Club he was often to be heard expounding on the virtues of the trumpet, which was his instrument; he could play 'When the Saints Go Marching In' and 'On Ilkey Moor Baht 'at', along with a few carols, and that was his limit. But he had a keen bunch of musicians who were much better players that he, and they pretended that he was conducting them, just to humour the old bloke.

Rehearsals went ahead, as the Feast was only three weeks away, and as preparations began in earnest, Norrie typed up his talk and set up a little old-fashioned lantern lecture, while Albert conducted the band and told the local teachers what costumes were needed for the floats.

With a week to go, Albert gathered all concerned in the club and lectured them about what was needed.

'Now, sithee ... the float ... we have four wagons and a motor-bike and sidecar. Float one is the medieval peasant shooting a deer; float two is the local monastery being sacked by old King Henry … '

'Wait a minute … wait a minute, Albert Peddle!' It was Norrie, about to question the plans.

'Some difficulties, Mein Fuhrer … one, we have no deer and two, since Tommy Mepp died there's nobody fat enough to be Henry the Eighth!'

'Well, first of all, Mr Know-All,' responded Albert, spluttering beer across the table, 'we might not have a deer, but there's Billy Crabtree's lurcher. We mun dress him up like a deer.' The assembled crowd laughed at that, and Albert ignored them. 'Then,' he went on, 'then … regarding chubby blokes … there's thee, Norrie Hissop … that must be fifty inches round that tub!'

Norrie was not willing to lose in this public confrontation. He pulled in his stomach and said, 'Forty-two inches … same as when I were thirty! As for the lurcher … he's of a nervous disposition and likely to bite any bugger what tries to put a deerskin on him!'

'Tha's just being awkward, Norrie Hissop! Thee leave it all to me and just concentrate on your boring little talk.'

Fate often stepped in to put a cloud over Albert's sunny days, and this Feast time was no exception. With two days to go, and the band and the pageant all ready, and the side-shows set up, after the wagons and carousel had trundled into Gawpham and set up on the village green, Albert took a risk. He knew it was a risk, but he ventured with a foolhardy attitude, to take part in a cricket match between the club and The Malt Shovel at Kittleworth. He was a useful fielder and could catch with one hand. He was put out by the boundary at long-field, as the Kittleworth opening batsman was known to be adept at doing delicate little chips off the side of the bat and sending the ball hurtling over the wicket-keeper.

The theory was correct, and the opening bat moved forward and caught the ball on the edge, sending it towards Albert. Now, when young, he would have thrown himself into the air and caught such a shot with one hand while his body was at full stretch; that was fine in 1928, but in 1955, when he tried to perform the same move, it was disastrous. He shot into the air and the crowd gasped; then he caught the ball, but went down on the green with a terrible thump and someone shouted out, 'Bloody hell.. I heard a bone crack!'

Uncle Albert was soon surrounded by the full medical resources of Gawpham: Mrs Winterbottom applied mouth-to-mouth resuscitation, because he was out cold; Willis tested his brother's limbs for movement and said, 'He's broken summat ... fetch Dr Bender!'

An hour after the accident, Albert was in the doctor's surgery, bandages applied to his leg. He lay moaning with pain, and lamenting his tragic situation.

'By heck, just when we were all ready for t' big day! God has it in for me, Doctor!'

Dr Bender tutted and sent him home to bed. 'Nothing is broken, but ligaments are damaged, and any forceful movement will do irreparable damage. Complete stillness and rest. You stay in your bed until I say you can go out ... or even move any part of you, do you hear, Mr Peddle?'

He said nothing, but nodded glumly and asked for some whisky, as a pain-killer.

By the evening he was wrapped up, moaning, and giving orders about the pageant and the band. Alice looked after him and he was molly-coddled with soup, cake and sympathy.

The first day of the Feast arrived, and there was Albert, early on that morning, just as the sun rose, in bed imagining what was happening out there – without him. The clock ticked on, and he heard excited gabbling and singing, then music and dancing, and he knew that if he didn't try to get there, he would always regret it. He had been banned from leaving the room, and if he tried to go downstairs and run for it … or limp for it … he would be grabbed and stopped by the tough and uncompromising Alice. There was only one possibility: to get through the window and escape onto Low Fold that way.

He made a supreme effort to get out of bed, slipped on his old trousers and shoes, and his usual mucky white shirt, and then pulled the sash window up, as silently as he could. He looked down. There was a drop of about ten feet. He had done that before, and he could do it again, so he gritted his teeth – all six of them – and went down to the cobbles. He gave an agonised yelp as his legs hit the hard stone, and then limped his way down to the Old Road by the club. Slowly, with a stab of pain at every move, he worked his way over the hundred yards, going closer and closer to the wonderful music of the carousel, and he could hear the brass band playing 'When the Saints …' without him!

As he reached the Old Road, he took two steps, and at that second, when he paused to gather strength for the next step, he tumbled over and lay in the middle of the road, stretched across, long-ways; as he lay helpless, he heard the unmistakeable sound of a cart coming along, at a trot, and he glanced up to see a man sitting atop the cart, which had a great strong horse pulling it. The man saw him but it was too late to move, and Albert, lying on his back in terror, shut his eyes and winced as the horse went over him, his hooves missing Albert's limbs; then followed the cart, and Albert said afterwards in the club, that St Jude, the patron saint of hopeless cases, was looking after him that day, because as the cart went over him, the side with the man's weight was not above his body.

The cart stopped, and the driver jumped down and stood above him.

'You daft bugger, why are you lying there in t' road?'

'I fell over, you clout-head!' Albert struggled to his feet and hobbled on to the Feast. What he didn't know was that the cart-wheel had left a deep and dark line of muck, running all the way down from one shoulder to the waist.

Norrie Hissop was just beginning his talk in the main tent, and the audience were lined up on benches, at six o'clock. He shuffled some papers and began. 'Ladies and gentlemen, my subject this evening is the history of our little village, here in the West Riding of Yorkshire, the county of Broad Acres, home of Captain Cook and Emily Brontë ... now what about the name itself? Well, it comes from the Anglo-Saxon for little settlement by the River Gaw, which you can hear if you listen very carefully, rippling and flowing not far from here. In the early days, it was the centre of the drovers' routes through here and their wagons would have been regularly trundling through the village ... '

At that point, Uncle Albert burst in, parting the flaps of the tent-door, and limped into the middle of an aisle. 'He's telling lies ... it's named because of the gawps who made pig-meat!'

He turned to face the audience, and someone cried out, 'Hey, Mr Hissop ... looks like the drovers are still trundling through here ... one's just trundled over Albert Peddle!'

Albert was soon, like the harvest, gathered in, and put back to bed. It took Alice an hour to clean the mud off him, and he was reminded over and over again, for weeks, that if the man had been sat on the other side of the cart, well, there would have been no more Uncle Albert.

Uncle Albert and the Trip to Filey

NOW, UNCLE ALBERT HAD A PASSION for food, and he had his particular favourite dishes. Rabbit soup was his daily dinner-time feast, with the boredom being relieved sometimes by mushroom soup, with all soups accompanied by huge chunks of bread, baked by Alice. It was always said of him, in a tone that was meant as a compliment, 'He never asked for much.'

But when holidays came around, it was always by the sea, and the sea meant crabs. He adored home-made crab paste and onion sandwiches, and so the seaside jaunts were *almost* always a real pleasure, but on one occasion that dark star of Fate hovered over Albert's pleasure.

That particular year a decision was made by Albert and his three brothers, along with their families, to have a week on the Yorkshire east coast at Filey. They chose the smallest shed of a place to stay, so that money was saved for beer and ice-cream. That meant a diet of beans on toast from the Calor Gas stove, and lots of take-away fish and chips. The caravans grew smaller every year. The smallest ever was a green dome the size of a pantry called 'Rosie' and the largest was a converted railway carriage (or part of one). These were all at Primrose Valley, next door to Butlin's holiday camp. But the family didn't need redcoats: they had Albert and his brothers, Willis and Fred.

A whole tribe of Peddles went that year: Albert had no small children, but Willis had two and Fred had three. The only properly viable way to get to the coast was in Fred's coal lorry. Economy was the word then, and fifteen people on the lorry was a hell of a lot cheaper than the whole gang going on the train, however romantic that was in my mind. Uncle Fred had a pub in Morley and a coal business. He was an entre-preneur of the school of Pa Larkin from H. E. Bates. There was this monster of a lorry, grinding and growling through the B roads of Yorkshire from Morley to Filey. In the cab were packed Aunts Dot and Renee, cousin Sandra, Willis and of course Albert, along with Fred, who drove the thing. On the back, with nothing to cling to but packing cases and ropes, were the bairns. The only way to make sure that the brood of Peddles were safe was to fasten the smaller ones to ropes, tied to corner-posts, and to strap the bigger ones to the headboard behind the cab. As the lorry rambled steadily through the other side of Leeds, and then towards Beverley, the bairns sang and played games, starting with I-Spy but then getting progres-sively sillier so that by the time the lorry pulled in for comfort breaks and tea or pop and crisps, there was a high level of giddiness and also some very mucky urchins, because Fred had left a pile of coal-sacks for the passengers to lie on for comfort.

When the lorry pulled into the large inn (probably there since the coaching days), the drinkers at their ease outside enjoying the sunshine saw what must have seemed like a gypsy colony arriving. Kids teemed out, lusty for pop and crisps and adults, legs crossed and skin pale as if sea-sick from the journey, managed to smile at those who stared, and gave Yorkshire greetings.

'Have you anybody else strapped under t' truck?' Someone said.

'Aye ... but he's dangerous so we daren't let him out!' Uncle Albert joked.

The children were like characters from The Water Babies, coated in soot except for where tears or snot had trickled down their cheeks or chins.

Albert and brother Willis downed a glass or two of beer or barley wine, and that guaranteed an ever more raucous final leg of the adventure. They entered into the holiday spirit like two stage comedians. Aunty Dot, Willis's wife, after a snifter, would invariably sing her Salvation Army song, as she was a keen Warrior for God:

> There is a flag that I love best,
> of all the flags I know.
> Its colours yellow, red and blue
> It's just the flag for you ...

The other travellers must have been so relieved when the party left the car park for the last leg of their journey to the sea.

By dusk, the lorry was at the camp-site and the three families jammed into two caravans. Economy dictated that one caravan for each family would have been far too expensive, and would have eaten into the beer money and the joint fund reserved for ice-creams. By nine, everyone had sat down to cheese and onion sandwiches outside one caravan, with a certain haste, because the men had their eyes fixed on the pub across the field.

Sleep that night was long and heavy, and eyes were rubbed, beans and toast gobbled, and washes all done skimpily in the promising morning, when the sun thankfully peered over the North Sea. The beach called and the expedition set off, with buckets and spades carried by the kids, wind-breaks and sandwiches carried by the men, and clothes and towels by the women. Albert had a special licence though: he had his elderberry wine, and his thoughts were on finding crabs.

Little Sidney was not aware of the strange habits of his Uncle Albert and asked about the wine and the tiddler-net that Albert carried.

'Well, lad, as a countryman, tha should know what mun catch a crab: it's Albert's patent Elderberry Knockout. I could have got rich on this if I'd framed myself when young.'

'Are the crabs drunk then?'

'You know what, you're dead right kid. The hunter finds a rock-pool, sees the crabs huddled up in a corner, and drops in a peck of elderberry wine, right? Then, oh do them there crabs get sleepy! In the hunter goes with the net ... repeat this ten times and by tea-time there's a bucket of crabs enough to feed all this mob of Peddles crab butties! See?'

Sidney thought that this would be half-right, as were most of his uncle's schemes, but he was prepared to wait and see.

Filey is notable for many things. It is a fishing village placed quietly in a sweeping wide bay between classy Scarborough to the north and busy Bridlington to the south; it appealed then – and still does – to those Yorkshire folk who clamour for a tranquil, traditional family holiday: arcade, boat-trips, beach games and fish and chips being the standard entertainment. Moreover, there is one special feature of the village that once had dozens of cobbles, small fishing boats, setting off from its shore: it has the Brig. This is a long, thin stretch of rock jutting out into the sea, providing a paradise for the holidaymakers whose idea of sheer bliss is to venture out, investigating rock-pools and collecting periwinkles and whelks, or of course, hunting crabs.

Everyone settled down, digging in and readying themselves for beach cricket first, and then after that there would be the swim and the daft games in the waves, followed by ice-creams. Everyone that is, except Uncle Albert, whose thoughts were on crab paste and onion sandwiches. He wore his usual dark blue suit and dusty brown boots, but made a concession to the holiday atmosphere by rolling up his trouser-legs and putting on his flat cap against the hot sun. His round, ruddy face, bewhiskered and moustached, was going to get browner as the week wore on, but he was due for a bad start.

In one hand he carried his large bottle of elderberry wine, and in the other his fishing net and a plastic tub for keeping the crabs in. This was one of the nets you buy for catching tiddlers or butterflies: a long bamboo stick with a small net on the end. He was tired by the time he reached the far end of the Brig, so he sat down by the first large pool he saw and took a swig of the elderberry wine. The pool was about six feet by four, and there should have been crabs a-plenty, but he could see none. The best ploy in this situation was to swirl the water around and disturb the creatures who were probably loitering under the rocks that jutted out at the pool's edge.

Albert plunged one hand in and there was a sharp spasm of pain as something nipped his finger-end. After his squeal of pain, which made some nearby pool-explorers laugh, he lifted his finger out and there was the crab, his first victim. He put it in his tub and put the lid on. 'I'll have you lot!' he said to himself, and dropped a splash of his wine into the water.

Then it became tedious. Nothing happened. No crabs emerged to be captured. Time ticked on, and he was thirsty, so he took a swig of wine. Time passed. He took another swig of wine, and another.

Seas have tides, and the North Sea at Filey is no exception. Tides ebb and flow, travelling in and out, in a cycle of fullness and distance. Not only do the great tongues of sea lick across the bay and leave golden sands; they swell in and leave nothing to see but the engulfing tide that smothers everything. That means even the solid rocky mass of the Brig would eventually be covered entirely by the sea, and on that afternoon, as always happens at such times, folk drift off, back onto the beach and into the walkways between the cliffs, so that gradually the Brig is left empty of people. On this day it was emptying fast, and most folk were aware of the advancing tide: but not Uncle Albert, who was dozing, because the main effect of having too much elderberry wine is sleep.

Fortunately, the family back on the beach saw that there was an empty space where Uncle Albert should have been, and that was at sandwich time; as Willis and Fred knew very well what Albert's weakness was (drink and gambling) they saw the advancing tide and ran off towards the Brig.

The cold water finally roused Uncle Albert, who shook himself, and noted the fact that he was lying in seawater so deep that he was automatically moving his arms, as if to start swimming. He was seen from a distance by his brothers, and they got to him at a perilous moment: he was in a gulley, and the water was washing over him now. 'Swim our Albert … move thyself now!' Willis called out, with a sense of urgency. Albert was swishing his arms around, but swimming had never been his strong point. He was lucky that Willis was ex-army and was prepared for the worst. He stretched out over the high rock and held out a hand. 'Your net ... stick the bamboo up. I'll grab it.'

The bamboo stick emerged and Albert was told to hold it like glue. He was not panicking, so that was an easy task.

Both brothers took hold of the end of the bamboo and tugged, and Willis, who had taken off his belt, lobbed it out so Albert could hold it with one hand and the stick with the other. In a minute or so he was out, in a desperate state, breathing heavily and holding his leg, and then catching at his backside with one hand and his leg with the other, as his brothers carried him, paddling knee-deep in sea water, back to safety.

They unloaded him onto the slope by the side of the yacht club, where the anxious family had gathered. As he lay there, gasping, everyone noticed that he had a crab fixing its claws to his behind and another with claws fastened on his knee. Although there was a general feeling of relief, their first urge was to laugh. The communal sound of a dozen Peddles all chortling and sniggering together, is enough to unnerve any man, and even Uncle Albert could not take it.

'There'll be no crab paste then Uncle Albert,' young Sidney said. 'They didn't like your elderberry wine.'

As he spoke, the empty bottle of wine rolled out of Albert's side pocket and down the slope. The great crab-hunter had no tub, no wine and no dignity.

'It's the last bloody time you'll get me coming to Filey Brig!'

And as he was still gasping for breath, Sidney spoke for all the kids when he asked, 'Is it Leeds Infirmary or sudden death, Uncle Albert?'

Uncle Albert and the Cellar

ALBERT'S BROTHER WILLIS lived to the south of Leeds at Beeston, a place of red-brick streets back in the fifties, with pubs on corners, picture houses in grand Art Deco style, and the jam factory, which was never short of work, being, as Gawpham was, in the heart of the famed 'Rhubarb Triangle' in the West Riding. Willis's house was in South Ridge Street, off the top of Beeston Hill, and the houses were roomy terraces: three storeys and cellars as well. Whenever Albert ventured up there, walking across open fields, it was with a feeling of elation and fun: he was always welcome and the children loved his company.

It was the cellars that caused the trepidation in this story, because whenever Albert went to visit Willis, there was the challenge of the cellars. Stairs leading down from the sitting-room led to the centre of the basement area, and to the left there was a food store, and to the right, a coal cellar. Across the top of the stairs there was a gate, made by Willis from odd bits of wood, as he was very useful in any craft or manufacture, and had made his living by making things, and even by inventing things, when need arose.

The gate helped to prevent accidents when the children played any rough games which might involve falling down the steps and doing themselves a serious injury. Downstairs, the food cellar was dominated by a massive cold slab, which looked like solid stone hewn from the side of some mountain. Willis called it a marble slab, but it was more likely granite, and his wife Enid kept her meat and cheese down there, putting glass cases over the food which was too tempting for any roaming vermin. Still, mice and rats did venture into there. An outside door led to the yard, and some steps outside led down from the main entrance door to the cellars. In the days before fridges were common, the food cellar was a dark, unnerving place at night, and that was the source of Albert's unease when he paid a call to enjoy playing cards and telling stories over a brown ale and home-made apple pie.

The cellar was the kind of place that somehow stood outside time: down there, it was wrapped in blackness, beyond everyday life, a place open to draw someone in like a fateful siren.

Albert was sure that the cellars were haunted, and Willis and family teased him about it. There was never any evidence of anything supernatural down there in the dark, but in Albert's mind there was a demon down there. Any tentative visit Albert might make when asked to go down and fetch some bread or cheese ended in him being nervous and as frightened as a 'daft bairn', as Willis said.

But one evening in autumn, when Albert was visiting, he had been promised a nice tasty tea of ham sandwiches and apple and blackberry pie with cream, and he arrived early, sat down to report on events in the village, and settle into a comfortable evening of good food and conversation. He knew, at the back of his mind, that the tormenting beggars were going to ask him to go to the cellar, and then have some fun at his expense, so he prepared himself mentally, steeling himself to cope with the challenge.

Time went on, and soon it was time to set the table and eat. Albert was in the old wooden kitchen chair with the thick cushion, rambling on about the war, his favourite subject, when Enid, standing there in the flowery pinny she wore every day, said, 'Hey, our Albert, would you be so kind as to go down and fetch that block of Cheddar cheese from the slab?'

Albert fastened onto his rising fear like a mastiff clamping on a bone, and nodded, making a false smile settle on his face, and he said, 'Of course, chuck. Cheddar you say?'

'Aye. On the slab.'

Enid looked at him. Willis looked at him. The three bairns, knowing full well that he was a coward in matters ghostly, looked at him, all searching his countenance for signs of fear.

'Right. I will then.'

'But there is one thing our Albert ... ' Willis said, softly and solemnly, 'You know that young Mrs Hannam at number six ... the one with the mental problems?'

'Aye ... . She was in an asylum wasn't she?' Albert asked, sensing something important being said.

'Well she was, yes. She came home last month ... but she's been in a funny way like lately.' Willis was hiding something, and Albert knew it.

'Funny way?'

'Aye, just doing odd things.' Willis was still keeping something back. Enid tried to make things clear. 'Yes, our Albert ... funny things. She ran out one day with a knife, like

41

... a carving knife. Very crazed look on her poor face, bless her.'

Albert took this in and planned what to do and say next. He was determined to maintain composure in the face of this disturbing news.

'She tends to ... well, to run out like, pulling at her hair and swinging that knife around!' Willis said.

'Surely she needs help. Couldn't she be recalled ... to the asylum I mean?'

'Well she's been in Meanwood ... they said she'd recovered after the treatment there, but I'm not so sure,' Enid went on, 'I mean, I saw her at the door the other day, pulling faces and screaming something about "*Get the demons out of me hair!*"'

Albert's silence continued. He was petrified but worked hard not to show it.

'Are you fetching that cheese, our Albert?' Willis asked.

'Aye ... of course. The cheese. Right away.'

He opened the gate. What follows was told later by Albert, in the bar of the club, and all who listened felt a cold shiver of fear run through them. This is how he told it a week later, in his beloved club, with his mates sitting listening.

'Well I opened that gate and went steadily down, step by step. As I got to the bottom step, I froze stiff, still as a statue, and listened. It was cold as the Arctic down there, and dark as the pit of Hell. The only light was a beam of moonlight thin as a pencil darting into the room and showing the top of a glass food-cover. I stood there, my eyes looking around for the cheese. All I could make out were the lumps and squares of the food and the bottles of drink on the big, broad slab.'

'What happened then?' asked Norrie Hissop.

'I took another step, and then stopped to listen again. Silent as the grave it was ... and as bloody cold. I heard a rustling noise from the corner, and I knew that was a mouse. But there was no other sound. I felt like every nerve in my body, every sense, every hair, was up straight listening for anything at all, from a breeze that might rattle the grille over the window, to a sound of that mouse eating a crumb. I put one hand out, feeling in the blackness of the cellar, for what food there might be there … '

'Did you find the ch … ch.. cheese?' old Harry Clemm, who had a stutter, asked.

'No. I felt some kind of packet. Then I stretched a bit further and my hand settled on something slimy … bacon I think it was. Now at that second I stopped because I had that sense … you know the feeling when you feel something or someone watching you? I had *that* feeling. Now, I turned around, ever so slowly, and fixed my stare on the far wall, between me and the coal-cellar, because I thought I heard breathing. It was a slow, deep breathing, and then as I looked closer, and took another step, there they were, staring at me!'

'Wh … what?' Harry Clemm asked.

'A pair of eyes, in that pitch black. The breathing was more of a rasping now, getting stronger. I found a scrap of courage from somewhere and I managed to find a few words. I asked, "Who are you?" Then, it moved. It shifted position and I heard a tapping noise, as if something was rapping on the wall. My heart was thumping up in my throat, as it said, "Free me!" I wanted to run for it, I'll tell you.'

'Didn't you hop it then, Albert?' Norrie asked, mesmerised.

'No. I had no need. There was a sound like as if a coat was being swished through the air and then … then the outside door opened and soon after it slammed shut.'

'Bloody hell! I'm a man of reason, but I wouldn't have swapped places with you for all the tea in China, Albert Peddle!' Norrie said, his voice betraying his nervous state.

Albert turned around, recovered himself, and it was then that he saw the block of Cheddar. He took hold of it, and ran back up the steps two at a time.

'Why by Heaven, Albert you look like … ' Enid said.

'Oh blood and sand, our Willis … I think I just met your mad woman!'

'Nay, that's impossible Albert. We were teasing you. She got taken back into Meanwood last week! Whatever you saw, it can't have been her!'

Uncle Albert and the Old Soldier

I T WAS ELEVEN O'CLOCK on a Saturday when young Sidney, who had been lying on the club wall waiting, saw Uncle Albert walking up the Old Road, and he ran to greet the old man. 'Hey, Uncle Albert … there's a man in there, he's been asking for you. Says he was in the war with you.'

Albert frowned and started wondering who it could be. He quickened his pace and followed the lad inside, to see a wiry, red-faced man holding forth to a gaggle of old-timers.

'Back to the action. We were expecting the next Big Push and my batman was peeing himself. There had been Big Push talk for three months and all we had were a few snipers, and that introduces one of my worst memories of the Big One. I'll tell you about that, but then I must press on to my imperial theme – the face-off with the Boche at Carie de Berges … '

'Another pint mister?' someone said, and the man nodded and wiped his lips, then went on:

'Now, the sniper – I was a little too bold this time; after taking a peep over the parapet I was sure all was clear and walked briskly along the trench with a whistle and a song. My aim was to taunt the buggers. To cap it, I swing spadger, my condom, in the air and of course the thing expanded somewhat with the centrifugal force. Gerry must have thought it was a chicken or something and he shot at it. Now, a spadger with a hole in it is bad news. The Madames check you out before there is any jig-jig allowed. There's a bulky big Frenchie on the door, solid as a bull, in case poor Tommy makes a stir of course.

'Spadger was manufactured by the best spunkus interruptus firm in the land, with best rubber to fit the member good and tight, but it couldn't stop a bullet. They had never been known to snap in moments of *oh ye Gods that'll do Miss* but a plug of lead cracks the whole John Company. The men were in fits at my dilemma of course, and I could hardly borrow another. This worried me for some time, as I had (and still have) the *call* once a week, normally on Thursday afternoon after beef.'

Here he stopped and saw that the fresh pint had arrived. He was relishing the completely spell-bound attention of his audience. Uncle Albert and Sidney were now in the doorway and Albert gazed at the man, trying to put a name to the face. Not wanting to ruin a good story, he let the man rattle on.

'I have no idea why I was rebuffed and scorned by my peers at school but so it was, and that's rather good training for the army life. At games I excelled at avoiding any participation, the reason being that all school physical exercise was focused on torture. The regime was meant to produce grafters at the great wheel of Empire, either pushing a pen or digging a hole, shooting the restless hordes or shifting weighty items of killing machines from A to B. I was destined to be a reject when young: my brain capacity was that of a flea, my stamina that of a sloth and my speed that of a grossly overweight pig.

All this meant that rather than go into a mill or on a farm I was sent to join the ranks of the Poor Bloody Infantry, and there I was, about to be killed by a damned sharp-shooter.

'Now I have never been one to show off, but it has to be said that I am one of a rare breed: those few rare bods who journey from squaddie to officer class. That means I rank with men such as Bill Robertson (a dear friend, and oh how I recall us hunting for boars in the wilds of the Punjab), a man who started as a nobody and was Field Marshall in the Big One. My progress as I write this has been to the rank of Colonel, and I haven't finished yet. Today I could have been a Field Marshall if it wasn't for Beefy Cottrell and that business with his daughter. I was never in her room and I was never anywhere near her person when she was allegedly touched and interfered with. Course, in the army word is spread like the clap in Gay Paree and heads turned, whispers were whispered and Cottrell saw to it that I would stay below tops in the pips league. Course, he's retiring in three months and I have laid schemes. Anyway, back to this sniper ...

'Now that's where Albert Peddle came in, your fellow village-dweller here in lovely Yorkshire ... yes, he saved my life. He gave out a blood-curdling scream and raced over No-Man's Land, ran up the bank and throttled the ruddy sniper to death! Yes, true as I'm sitting here now, he did for the Bosch ... and saved my good self ... so I've come to meet up with him and ... ' Here he gave a dramatic cough, 'Before I peg it and go to the great barracks in the sky. Now, could anyone tell me where I can find this hero?'

'I'm standing here ... who the hell are thee?' Albert stepped out into the light and confronted the visitor.

The man stood up, to his less than impressive height of five feet two inches, and he held out his hand. 'Schofield

Murgatroyd, King's Own Yorkshire Light Infantry, formerly ... in short, the good old KOYLI, and you are the man who saved my life! Bless you Albert ... after all these years!'

Albert, being good-mannered down to his bones, shook the man's hand but still had no memory of the name.

'Murgatroyd ... I don't recall your name I'm sorry to say, lad. I saved your life tha says?'

'Yes, at *Carie de Berges* ... when you killed that sniper.'

Now, Albert had always kept quiet about his days in the Great War. He was born in good Queen Victoria's reign and had signed up as soon as war was declared in 1914. Now here was this old chap, walking into the club in 1959, saying that Albert was a hero. It was too good an opportunity for free drink and glory to miss. He put on his best old comrade back-slapping act and went along with it.

Backs were slapped, memories recalled and beer consumed in huge quantities all through the dinner-time hours, through until three o'clock. In that time, more than thanks were given: Schofield took a small box from his pocket and gave it to Albert. When he opened it, there was a bullet, mounted on a gold stand. In was engraved with 'The second bullet would have been deadly, but for Pte. A. Peddle.'

But just before the landlord shouted for everyone to go home, in walked Norrie Hissop, hoping to have a swift half before closing time. He sat down with the drunken gang of old men, and he was told the story of the sniper yet again, in a spasmodic way, by Albert, as he had started to believe the tale told by Schofield. Finally, the visitor shook hands for the last time, and took his leave, promising to call in again if God willed.

'Now, tha's an historian Norrie ... listen to this. This old soldier what's been here ... he was at *Cary Debinge* with us like, and well, this … this sniper … he … well, I killed the beggar!'

'You never told us this before, Albert? Shy are you? Modest?'

'Well you keep it in don't you? War is taboo, like. We should forget and, and … and have … peace like!' He hiccupped and almost fell off his chair.

Norrie's mind was sifting through the events of the war and recalling Albert when young. A thought then struck him. 'But Albert … what about that service record?'

'Service record? Whassa mean?' (hic).

'Well, you remember, when I did that little booklet about Gawpham folk … it showed tha were in t' hospital most of 1916. You missed the Somme.'

'Oh the Somme, aye … but I were there at Cary Debinge.'

'Albert … Carie de Berges was an engagement in the Somme battle.'

The truth then dawned. Albert's mouth dropped as he saw what had happened. 'Oh, blood and sand … our Arthur … he was in the KOYLI as well. He copped a bullet at Mametz Wood!'

'Aye, and he was a proper soldier!' Norrie said, with an indignant tone. But there was Uncle Albert, running his thick fingers over the bullet, and thinking. 'Oh so this was meant for our Arthur, God bless him, who never came back … well bugger me!'

'Now what Albert? That thing must go to the museum at Forley.'

'You're joking old lad … It says on it "Pte A. Peddle" – it'll do for me.'

Every Christmas after that, out came the bullet, and Albert told the tall story to give everybody a laugh. He put on Schofield's voice and began,

'Now, I've never been one to show off, but it has to be said that I'm one of a rare breed: those few rare bods who journey from squaddie to officer class ... and anyway, one day in the hell of the Somme, there was this sniper ... '

Every time he told the tale, Albert said a little prayer to his brother Arthur, asking forgiveness for the bit of fun.

Uncle Albert and the Deaf Quarryman

IN HIS YOUNGER DAYS, between the wars, Albert was a quarry gaffer. That meant he bossed everybody in the big stone quarry at Forley. It was a hard way to make a living, because great square rocks of stone had to be taken out of the quarry-face, and that was after the men had used dynamite to blast a massive chunk of rock and earth out of the side of the quarry basin, and that basin was so wide you could put half of Gawpham in it. The story goes that one of Albert's closest brushes with death, when he was only a pin-head away from meeting his Maker, came in that quarry.

It started with the day two young men came to his quarry office, seeking work. Now, this was in the 1930s when times were very hard for folk. Jobs were few and far between, and a number of families around Gawpham and Kittleworth were in very dire straits. Albert was at that time a youngish married man himself, and he had some sympathy with unemployed chaps.

The two men stood outside his office, which was a rough sort of cabin about the size of a caravan, and one was broad and well muscled, with an old, ragged pair of trousers on his thin frame, and a blue shirt full of holes, while his friend was tall and thin, with a mop of ginger hair, and he wore a blue overall so he looked like a man who was useful with his hands. The shorter one did the talking.

'Morning gaffer ... we was wondering if you had any work, like?'

'Has tha done quarry work before?'

The same one answered, 'Not exactly quarry work ... but I have fired guns, in the Royal Artillery.'

That impressed an old sweat like Albert, who thought that army men were trustworthy. But he was still cautious.

'I don't need any workers for ordinary work, but if tha could blast maybe?'

The shorter one nodded and the tall one smiled and copied his friend, nodding even more vigorously.

'Well it's three bob a week for starters ... come tomorrow at eight. I'm Mr Peddle by the way, who are you two?'

The same man answered; still the tall one said nothing. 'I'm Harry and this is Maurice.'

'Right. See you tomorrow', Albert said, and they trailed off into the distance.

The next morning there they were, standing by the cabin. They wore the same clothes. Albert called his foreman across. 'Na then, Syd, get these two busy putting sticks in number four hole. We're taking fifty yards out this morning.'

The foreman was completely committed to his work, and as he led them across to the little tunnel where they would place the dynamite, he gave them a lecture.

'Now see ... tha's done this afore?' The smaller one nodded and his friend nodded after him. 'Right, well then, if tha don't know this area, let me say that most buildings around here have fronts from this quarry ... ashlar and millstone ... it'll last for ever lads ... well past me and thee on this earth. Take Forley Town Hall for instance – seen that classical frieze with the men working with shovels? Go and have a butchers at it – it come from here. Stone from here is at colleges and halls all over the place ... Technically, we're in what the geologists call the Middleton Grit Group ... are tha listening?' He turned to look at them. The shorter one nodded and the second one copied him, and nodded again.

'Here we are. I'll leave thee to it. Put three in there, where I've marked it, and three over there – see that chalk cross? Then bugger off quick as a rat with a Jack Russell up its backside, right?'

The foreman walked off, after opening the box of dynamite and putting six sticks into a thin metal-lined container, which he passed to the shortest lad.

At that point, just as the shortest lad gave his friend three sticks to put in the marked cross, and he himself went to the other marking, back at the cabin, Albert had been worrying about the job, as he always did, and so he walked slowly towards the work-face, meaning to check up on everything. As he came near, he met the short one, coming out quickly.

'Where's your mate?' Albert shouted.

'I thought he come out!' The lad said.

Albert said that he panicked, and ran into the tunnel opening to be sure that the lad was out. But no, there he was, still crouching by a rock-face. Albert shouted, but there was no reply.

'He won't hear you ... he's deaf and dumb, my mate, mister Peddle!' The short lad called.

Albert wanted to grab the two lads and smack their heads together, but he had first to get the dumb one out. He sprinted to him, pulled his jacket, and as he turned, he pointed to the open air and made a shape with his arms to show an explosion. The dumb lad didn't wait for any more explanation: he was out of there, with Albert behind him, in a split-second.

The two lads were behind a rock before Albert, who was slower than they were. He took the little tail-end of the blast, and fell down on his face.

'I were always a bit deaf myself after that,' he said, 'and my interviews with workers were a bit more thorough after that. But I'll never forget the young tall lad's face when he said thank you ... he yanked my arm up and down and there was a beam on his face like Harpo Marx.'

Uncle Albert and the
Fire Station Ghost

RESTLESS SPIRITS SEEMED TO ATTRACT ALBERT. He was full of unearthly stories, and some said he had a sixth sense. The most unnerving tale he told was from the war years, and it led to him accepting a challenge and a bet.

Back in the Second World War, Uncle Albert helped out by working with the fire service, as he was too old to fight and he didn't like the thought of drilling with the Home Guard. But he regretted his decision, after one night at Kittleworth Fire Station, when something from the other world paid a call.

It happened one night when the men were doing a few jobs and cleaning the equipment; Albert was there as they worked in the old appliance room, which survived from an earlier building now partly demolished. It was the custom of the officers to go through the ritual of essential tasks before sitting down to have a chin-wag and listen to the radio. The last job of the day was to lock the side door. There was an external alarm bell for the general public to ring if an emergency arose.

That night, there was a gale blowing outside, and the wind had its feelers in every little corner, every alcove, every collection of tins and boxes, in that packed little station. At first, when the strange events began to happen, some thought of the bad weather, and put it down to that. But other things happened soon enough.

Albert said that after the jobs were done, they sat down, and their kit was hung on the wall. One man was making a model galleon, and the largest piece of wood, about a foot long, was thrown inexplicably across the room, slamming into the opposite wall. But then, footsteps were heard outside and approaching the side door. Everyone heard the footsteps as they were talking, and they seemed to come into the building. The Sub Officer accused a man of not locking the door, but they all waited to see what was going on.

Albert continued the tale:

'We all went still as we saw the lock turn as if there was a key in it, outside ... then these footsteps came into the main room, and then slowly padded along the stone slabs of the corridor. We all listened and stared, our heads moving along with the movement of these feet ... . On the footsteps went, across a yard and up some steps to a locked store-room which had dangerous substances in it. The lads were, of course, shaking with fear. I saw their heads turn, as I dipped under the table, not wanting to risk being there if it was something evil ... and we felt the floor shake slightly to the sound of these ghostly footsteps, across the room, slowly up the stairs, and then the handle on the door was rattled.

'I was with big, strong men, fearless against the terrors of fire and smoke, but they shivered with fear that night, roused from a friendly atmosphere and the homely sound of the radio, to witness something uncanny. I don't know what the hell it was. But the story goes, as we heard after, that a man, years back, had been blown to pieces by handling some chemical, and his spirit was heard going to the place where he died. I'm not ashamed to say that I was under the table when the other blokes finally stood up and walked across to the steps to see what they could find as evidence of anything that might have been disturbed.'

That was the first taste of the spirit the men had dubbed Old Tom. But one of Albert's weaknesses was that he could never resist a bet. After he came out from under the table, he was ribbed and teased, and one man, Jimmy, said, 'I'll bet you five quid you can't stay in here on your own through one night!'

Some little voice inside urged Albert to find an excuse for what they'd heard. 'Well, there's the old workshop upstairs, and what with the wind blowing, and all the old bits and pieces of tools up there, it was something that fell on the floor above ... sounded like footsteps but it wasn't! That's the explanation right enough. Then there's the wind ... you've heard the gale out there ... enough to dislodge Big Ben I'd say!'

'Come on then – five quid!' Jimmy said again.

Without a thought, Albert accepted, but there was one problem. 'It'll be a night shift though, so what about the crew?'

'We can stay next door ... this old room is plenty big enough for you ... and that way we can be sure that you've not sneaked out, Albert!'

He had no way to wriggle out now. His heart went into palpitations when he just thought about it, but a night was chosen, only two weeks after the footsteps had paid a visit, and Albert had to get settled into the old appliance room, and wait for his visitor.

He had talked himself into believing that there was a rational explanation for the noises that night, and that the room above was so full of objects that some of them must have been dislodged that windy night. But he had to pass the time, and he had to keep busy, so that the hours would tick by more quickly. The lads were next door, and he knew that they would be checking up on him, even listening at the door. He started off playing solitaire, and then he made tea. All the while, one eye was on the door, waiting for the footsteps.

Then, at around three in the morning, as he sat with a blanket over his knees, the alarm bell rang next door. There was the usual clatter and shouts, as the lads ran to get dressed and gather the equipment. The great wooden doors were swung open and someone shouted, 'Get a move on – fire at the clothes factory on Crimea Street – look sharp!'

In a few minutes he was all alone. There would be nobody next door. Who would ever know, he thought, if he slipped out and kept well away from that haunted room? He told us what happened.

'Well, I crept out … into the main, new rooms, and helped myself to some sandwiches that were lying around. The lads were out fighting a blaze and I was all right, mate, everything dandy. Until that is, I dropped off and fell asleep, and time passed, the crew came back, saw me, and dug me in the ribs to wake me up. It was eight in the morning.

'So … did you last out the night, Albert?' they all asked.

'Yes, no problem at all! Nothing happened in there – I've just come out', I said, and oh God, how wrong can you be? One of the lads opened the door into the old appliance room and we heard a cry of amazement. 'Come here quick lads!' he said.

'We all trailed in, gob-smacked at what was in front of us. The door to the store up the steps was open and across the whole expanse of the broad floor there were strewn containers of every kind of dangerous substance you could imagine. They all looked at me.

'Five quid you owe me … you couldn't stick it … and look what it's done in here!' Jimmy said, holding out his hand.

Albert said that never again after that did he doubt that there was another world somewhere stuck in the middle of ours, and restless, haunted souls lived in that space. 'Tha meets these ghouls and demons when tha least expects it … like that night in the appliance room … and the worse thing was that when we cleared up, we found an identity card lying on the floor in the corner … it was the dead man's … and tha knows what was odd about it?' Albert asked the listeners as he sat in his corner seat at the club, 'Well, the face on the card was blurred, like as if something had smudged the face out.'

Uncle Albert and the Hot Tip

L ONG AGO, BACK IN THE FIFTIES, people in Gawpham led the lives of traditional English villagers as they had throughout the centuries, and although changes came and went as Father Time ground on regardless, fundamentally not much affected the steady course of life. When Elizabeth II came to the throne, people in her Yorkshire community centred on the Working Men's Club did much the same as they did when other monarchs had been and gone. Mrs Barber collected firewood; Norrie Hissop researched the life of Sir Hereward Bean, Lord of the Manor in the fourteenth century; the Slacks ran around the back court by the midden like mice in straw, and Albert Peddle backed the wrong horse.

That's what Albert had always done. He had to have a flutter every day, and sixty years ago, a man could invest bets in sums of sixpence (half a shilling and in modern terms, two and a half new pence). His betting slips were filled in as he sat in the club, and sent to his brother-in-law who worked in a betting office somewhere in Leeds. There were no betting shops for most of Albert's life, so for many wagers, when he had no slip and wanted to bet on the spur of the moment, he had George Backhouse's bag.

George was the bookie on the move. He was small, always wrapped in a long black coat and wore a black bowler hat. He was consequently often mistaken for the undertaker. Now, George would saunter into the club, order a glass of pale ale and sit quietly in a corner with his big black leather bag across his knees. Folk then went sneakily and discreetly to him, in order to place a bet. A man would sidle up, say from the corner of his mouth, 'Two bob … Greek Warrior, two-thirty at Warwick' and hand over the two-shilling piece.

That was all normal practice, but there was much more to it, because George Backhouse knew a number of professionals in the Sport of Kings. This meant something very important to punters such as Uncle Albert, who normally spent several hours every morning studying the form in *The Racing and Football Outlook*. Working with the paper made the game all about form. That was all very well up to a point, but there were variables in the real racing game. A horse might be poorly on the day of the race; he might have a cough or he might feel more like a nap than a sprint. A punter needed to know these extra little details.

That's where George came in, because George was Alice's uncle. Family members were expected to share information. Of course, such matters had to be handled with sensitivity and discretion. George used signals to convey such crucially important equine details. When he sat down, those in the know (Albert and Fred mainly) would watch for his big finger going up to scratch or rub his right eyelid, as if he was tired or had a sore eye. That meant that he had information concerning a tip from the stables about a horse that was expected to win.

As time went on, George developed his own tic-tac signals – a whole range, similar to the tic-tac semaphore used at the tracks to show a horse's starting price. But if he rubbed his eye, Albert and Fred knew that the name of the horse would be written on a beer-mat at the bar just before George left. The brothers could then put their bets on and take some cash from George's rival bookies.

There was another system in place as well. This referred to the big races, such as the classics, when information was needed well in advance, because folk backed their horse ante-post, months or weeks before the race. That gave them longer odds, often backing a horse at 20–1 which would start on the day of the race at 4–1.

As Albert, since the age of fifty-five, had never done a full day's work, he relied on a whole range of little plans and ploys that would keep beer-money trickling in. But it was all a risky business, and times could be lean. Sometimes a month would pass without Albert selling any rabbits from his shooting with Timmy, and without vegetables being sold from Alice's garden.

Such a time was in the spring of 1954. Nothing had sold for weeks. He was thinking desperate thoughts; he even considered offering to help Mrs Barber collect firewood from Panley Copse, but in the end, he decided, as he ran his few coins through his hand, that he would have to ask the landlord for a pint on tick and then go back a winner to gather some wealth again. He got the tick, so then he owed the landlord a total of two pounds and he had a dirty look from the man as Albert's pint was pulled.

'This is the last one, Albert … I'm not a charity, old lad!'

'No, course not. I'm no scrounger either. I've a lucky feeling coming on.'

'It's not in your water is it? Folk say they can feel stuff in their water … '

'Nay lad … my water's all Tetley's bitter.'

He was bluffing. Albert was at the end of his tether in fact. Then, fate intervened, as George Backhouse walked in, ordered his glass of pale ale at the bar, gave Albert a wink, and went to sit down. Sure enough, as he sat, Albert saw his pokey little scrawny finger go up and rub his eye-lid. Albert gave a great sigh of satisfaction, watched George finish his glass and walk to the bar with the empty, and write on the beer-mat.

When George left, Albert was there in a flash. There it was, written in the usual scribble. Albert, screwing up his eyes, could just make out the word 'Wellington'. He checked his paper, and saw that Wellington was running in the four o'clock at Doncaster.

His only problem was that all he had in the world to back the horse with, was twelve shillings. But he sent a kid running with the money and the slip to the little office behind number ten Inkerman Street and the bet was on.

That night, at seven, into the club rolled Albert, some fivers in his hand and his face beaming. He paid off his tick to the landlord and bought drinks for his mates. When George came in, he got a double whisky and a pat on the back.

'Trainer passed the word on to Tiny Sidebottom, and Tiny gave the whisper to Harry at the Co-op, and then Harry whispered the name to my mate Peter, and then Peter told me. The message was: "*Wellington boots it today ...*"'

A few weeks passed, and Uncle Albert did all his usual little bits of business: Timmy brought in three birds, and Albert earned five bob cleaning the tractor at Hereward Bean's farm. Alice had been baking for three days solid so there was food on the table and to spare, but the beer-money was all spent. It was time to get down the club and wait in hope. It turned out to be a fateful day for Albert: the weather was foul, and as he walked down the Old Road, a straight Roman road that had been there unchanged for all those centuries since the legions left, the gusts of wind blew up the dust and the leaves, and everyone walking about had to wrap their coats around them, even though it was the middle of May.

Albert settled in the club and started studying form. If George didn't turn up, then there would have to be some serious concentration on the race-cards and he would have to rely on skill. But at half past one, in came George. He walked to the bar, gave Albert a sideways wink, took his glass of pale ale to the table, and sat there, bag across his knee. Punters sidled up to him and he was busy this time. The local betting men were in a mood to get an early bet on for the Derby, which was in early June. The papers had been full of talk about Carolina, making it seem a certainty, and its price was 2–1.

Word had got around that George would be opening his bag for ante-post bets on the big race, and so he was popular. Albert kept looking across, and time and time again George put his finger to his eye-lid and rubbed.

'By heck, this must be a red-hot one … ' Albert whispered to Fred, 'He's rubbed his eye a dozen times, old lad!'

Then when the punters had all finished, there was one last rub of his eye before he walked to the bar and in half a minute he was out of the place.

Albert was there like a whippet, looking for the beer-mat. But there was a problem: there were about a dozen beer-mats. He asked the landlord for a pint to keep him distracted, and flipped the mats up and down, and there at last was a scribbled name: *Wellington boots it today* … It was the same horse as last time.

Albert took it on trust, and by Derby Day he had five pounds to win on Wellington, which had won for him before, and now was tipped to win again. He sat by the radio in the sitting-room and his heart thumped with excitement. Five pounds was a great deal of money then, and he stood to win seventy if it came in the winner.

They were off, and there was Wellington, clearly well behind, at the back. The field went on and on, past the mile post, and Wellington was still at the back. 'Still four furlongs to go ... it'll come with a late run!' Albert said. But in the closing stages, the horse was still struggling at the back. He had kissed goodbye to his fiver.

That night, in the club, when George came in, Albert was straight over to him and fixed him in the eyes: 'You bloody fool ... that tip for t' Derby ... came in last!'

'What tip?'

'Wellington of course.'

George's face creased ready to laugh, 'You daft ha'porth ... I didn't leave no tip.'

'Tha did ... I saw thee rub that eye ten times!'

'Aye, because I had some grit in it!' George reminded everybody that the day he was in the club it had been blowing a blizzard outside. 'There was so much muck about, I had half of the fields in Gawpham in my eye that day, you wassock!'

Enlightenment came to Albert as he saw what had happened. The man to blame was the landlord, old Ken. He was over there in seconds, to tell him off. 'Ken ... change them bloody beer-mats more than once a year. Tha's cost me a fiver!'

Uncle Albert and the Coal Hole

ALBERT'S BROTHER WILLIS, as has been explained, lived in Beeston in his large terraced house. In the height of the war with Hitler, when the Blitz raged and the Nazis were after smashing the ordnance factory, just a mile or so downhill from Beeston Hill, Albert paid one of his rare visits to his brother, supposedly to play cricket in the park with the children, but really it was to share some home-brewed beer that Willis had made as an experiment.

Albert, notorious as a man with a stomach of steel, who had been known to scoff a dozen baking apples and a bunch of rhubarb freshly picked and without sugar, relished the thought of a potent home-brew, and he arrived one late afternoon in 1941, without a thought in his mind about the war that was going on, enjoying his day off from his work in the fire brigade.

He was aware that he and the cellar of number fourteen, South Ridge Street, did not agree: in fact, he felt a shiver of terror when even a fleeting thought of that gloomy place passed through his mind. With that in mind, he was determined not to spend time in the house, but to go to the pictures for the evening, before staying the night and setting off to walk the mile back to Gawpham next morning.

A night at the pictures was perfect, except that he went with Willis's sister-in-law Grace, who was notoriously difficult, and he had the feeling that she had been pushed to go with him by Willis and his dear wife, to get her out from under their feet. Grace was, they said, highly strung. What that really meant was that she had a mind of her own and wanted more out of life than knitting and sewing, and talking about film stars. But she did love the flicks, and off she went, with Albert and Mrs Appleby from next door, to provide a moral presence.

Things went swimmingly until the film, which was a dark, historical one involving some Cossacks and a band of Slavic brigands, built up to a scene of torture. Albert and his two lady companions prepared themselves for the worst as two evil-looking henchmen made ready to squeeze the eyeballs out of their prisoner, who stood firmly and took it like a man. Grace became restless: she was very imaginative and had suspended her disbelief to such a degree that she was restless, and started muttering something under her breath.

'Hey lass,' Albert said, 'it's only a film … them's onions, not the bloke's eyes!'

But it was to no avail. Grace rolled in her seat, and then stood up, in the pitch-black and screamed, 'You bad buggers … leave him alone!'

The manager arrived, with a burly assistant, and the three of them were escorted out of the picture-house. 'I was only getting involved in the story!' Grace protested.

As they walked out onto Beeston Hill the air-raid warning started, its horrible drone pulsing through the streets, planting seeds of sheer panic in everyone's hearts. Albert thought quickly, 'Now then ... there's a shelter up Hanvill Street ... we can get there instead of going to the one in your street.' They walked at top speed and after turning a few corners, they saw before them the Hanvill Street shelter and made for it. As they parted the thick cloth over the entrance, the line of people squatting alongside the inside seats gave them a hard stare.

'Do you belong here? You're not one of us!' their leader said.

'We'll not stay where we're not wanted ... but there is a war on ... we could die out there!' Albert said.

'Oh right-o ... utch up everybody and let 'em in!' the leader said.

After the utching up, as bottoms slid further along the seats to make room, the folk in the shelter warmed to their visitors and suggested a sing-song. Albert always loved that and he was first in with his Al Jolson impression of 'Mammy' and he was the cause of great hilarity. Back then, people adored the blacked-up minstrels, an act that had been popular since the mid-Victorian times, and nobody thought it racially offensive.

'Hey that was good mister ... shame you can't black up!' one of the shelter-people said.

Time went on, and bombs were heard not so far off, nearer the centre of Leeds. Someone suggested a prayer, and heads were bowed. After that it was jokes and stories, and finally, it was back to 'Mammy'. The siren stopped, and Grace asked the time, and when told it was ten, she ran out and said she had to be back home. Mrs Appleby ran after her.

Albert, following, shouted for them to be careful, as the blackout was still on and it was dangerous to run in the thick, heavy darkness of the unlit night. Albert trod very carefully, slow step after slow step, pausing every now and then to be sure that he was heading in the right direction.

Eventually he saw that he was at the corner of South Ridge Street and Bennett Street and he knew that he was almost at Willis's house. He took a step forward and whoosh, down he went, into blackness. The world dissolved under him. In seconds he landed with a terrible thump on something very hard. He felt pain run through all his limbs and his head was spinning; for a while he lay there, looking up at a perfect round hole and the moon beyond.

Taking his bearings, he looked around and saw coal. He was in a coal cellar. After a while he struggled to his feet and walked gingerly towards the doorway. He put his hands to his face to rub bruises and clear his eyes of dust, and then, to his absolute horror, he saw that he was standing between the two cellars at Willis's house.

Bad memories assailed him, and he felt a deep panic down in his guts; all he wanted was to be out of there, so he made for the steps and went up those familiar stone stairs, emerging into the light of the sitting-room, where Willis and family were sitting having tea and biscuits, and Grace was talking about how they had been thrown out of the Malvern Picture House. No one was eating the pickled onions with the salad, as Grace had told them all about the Cossack being tortured. But Grace looked up from her food and grinned. 'Hey, Uncle Albert … you did black up … are you going to sing Mammy again?' Grace asked with a giggle. Albert, exhausted and wracked with pain, fell to his knees, but no one stopped laughing. They thought it was part of the act.

'I'd walk a million miles, for one of your smiles, my mameee … ' Willis sang. As for Albert, he vowed never to go to the pictures with young Grace ever again.

Uncle Albert and the Gawpham Werewolf

TALK AT THE CLUB, at the end of the night, when men had been at their ease so long that their wits went soft as cardboard, turned to the subject of the supernatural. The rational men, such as Norrie Hissop, said 'Pooh ...' and made rude noises. Others were less dismissive, and some, like old Louis Codd, made it clear that he believed in every kind of undead it was possible to encounter. But there was a certain level of jollity, and that was too much for Uncle Albert, who cut in with the words, 'If tha knew what the real night were like ... tha'd not be so chirpy about restless souls!

'Go on then Albert ... tha's started it now', Louis said, nudging his old friend's elbow, and Albert began.

'In the old folk tales, there are yarns told about those horrible creatures made when a man turns into a wolf – yes, the werewolf. But one story is not to be ignored, lads ... it's about the creature that's worse than the rest, and it's a Yorkie tale of a beast special to our county – a particularly nasty type of dog-like creature called a *Lobhound*. I've had many an encounter with this hairy monster, and I could tell some blood-curdling tales about it. This lobhound was a species of werewolf.'

'Go on then – don't stop now!' Louis said.

'Right, you've asked for it, but get me a pint!' Albert warmed to the task. This is the tale he told.

One time, a man they called Deano, who was a carpenter, had been working hard all morning, and he had even been working in the night as well, at home, to make a shed for his tools, as he had to work hard to make ends meet.

Deano was one of these carefree, devil-may-care blokes; he wasn't fussed about how he looked because he wasn't interested in women or in looking nice. He always wore his red hat, a dirty shirt and trousers with holes in them. People used to joke that he never looked in the mirror, and even if he did he would think he looked great. Now, he was a friend of Albert's and Albert told this story about him, usually on a winter's night.

He was a loner, this Deano, except for his friend Albert. He had no wife or partner in his life, so he just worked and enjoyed a drink or two. His neighbour, Marisa, cooked for him and cared for him when she could, but she had her own life to lead. She was a married woman, and she lived next door, busy with her family, though she worried about her strange neighbour, and she told Albert about him.

Deano worked so much he hardly ever slept. He learned to get by without much sleep. But now, on this particular day, he was really tired and so he stopped for lunch. He ate his sandwich at the table in a nearby café, and he knew that he was so tired that he might not keep awake in the afternoon, so he took a few strong drinks. Uncle Albert, at Marisa's begging, sometimes went to sit with him, and try to get him to come down the club for a pint, but he wouldn't budge from his routine.

Then one day, Deano was walking back to work when the clouds gathered and it went very dark, and he was walking with Albert, after a chat, down a path where he could have a pee – it wasn't his usual route. He couldn't explain it, but he felt strange. It seemed as though some kind of shadow passed over him and he shivered. He couldn't explain what was happening. Albert said he was worried, and stayed with him, and when the lad felt better, Albert walked with him, back to work.

As they were sitting back in his workshop, Albert saw Deano turn a strange colour and begin to sweat, unnaturally. Suddenly, Deano said, gripping his work-bench, day began to feel like night, and he felt strange. A feeling came over him like he was being possessed, invaded by something. He looked at his hands and he saw that they were growing hair. Then he felt his face change and his jaw was bigger. Soon he was bending forwards and he started making howling sounds.

Albert got out of there fast, and went for a drink or two, saying nothing about what he thought he had seen: he couldn't see how it really could have happened, and he thought he was going daft through too many late nights.

Marisa was worried when her neighbour was not seen for several days, though. Then it got weird. Folk around Gawpham said they were scared of a werewolf that was running around – and some said that it had Deano's clothes on. What could Albert do but take some advice? His friend wasn't a werewolf – surely not? But the more the reports came, the more he was sure that it had to be true. Now, there was only one thing to do, and Albert, whenever he had a brush with the unexplained, had somewhere to go. He decided to go and see Mrs Haddock, a wise old woman who lived in an ancient ruin of a house, crumbling and full of mice and birds, on the edge of the village. Long ago she had been a teacher and had a little school of her own, but she had met hard times. The rumour was that she sat up all night, reading old, leather-bound books full of ancient wisdom. The bairns in Gawpham were terrified of her.

'Your mate's a werewolf? Oh old lad, how terrible!' Mrs Haddock said. 'But don't worry, there are ways we can sort this out. Forget all that silver bullets and garlic stuff. Is he wearing any clothes? If he's wearing clothes we have a good chance we can get this bloke back.'

'Yes, he's wearing his checked shirt and black trousers – what he always wears. He must be my mate Deano.' Uncle Albert was upset just thinking about it. The man he had tried to help had now turned into some kind of freak.

'You mean he never changes his clothes? My husband was the same – men!' Mrs Haddock shrugged and moaned. 'Anyway, Albert, you can only destroy a *lobhound* – because that is what he is – by burning his clothes, but wherever he is, he'll smell and he'll come to get you to stop the burning – because he'll feel the heat – even if he's hundreds of miles away.'

'That sounds a bit rum … ' Albert said.

'You need to get his clothes while he's asleep and then take them somewhere to burn them, somewhere where there will be no smell of burning', Mrs Haddock explained.

Albert stroked his beard and his moustache. He was starting to wish he'd never got involved, and left Deano to his own resources. But there was a gram or two of charity in him, and he wanted to help the poor man. But the task seemed impossible. These wise women did talk some old rot, he thought to himself.

'What? You're kidding. How can you burn something without a smell of burning?'

Mrs Haddock screwed up her face, puzzled. 'You need to find a place that's sealed in, a place that not even a square millimeter of air can get in.' Mrs Haddock smiled. 'Quite a tall order I guess!'

'Oh, easy ... that'd be George Backhouses's wallet!' Albert joked.

That made Uncle Albert have a long think and then his brain came up with some ideas that were a bit cock-eyed, but maybe they would work. If he had to set to work to loosen his brain-cells, Albert usually went for a walk in his quarry when the day's work was done and he needed perfect quiet. The great chasm was ideal for thinking. There it was, towering all around him, steep-sided, with just little tufts of strong grass on the edges, and a few buzzards circling overhead in the grey sky. In a place like that you have big ideas, thoughts that would rattle the sides of the world like a spoon stirring a mug of tea.

Albert had to think of a place, somewhere airtight and man-tight ... and in fact, somewhere werewolf-tight. He thought of a few possible places. Their little village was full of dark, forgotten, crumbly corners where you could hide away and burn stuff.

But first he had to get Deano's clothes. He went in the daylight when werewolves do not move around and he looked for his den. He looked all over the hills and fields nearby but with no luck. Then, when he came close to Deano's house, almost in despair, he heard a snoring coming from the new shed that Deano had built the year before. It was the kind of snoring that a very big animal might make.

Uncle Albert crept to the shed and peeped through the window. There, lying on a camp bed, was the lobhound, fast asleep – a big hairy dog but with Deano's trousers, shirt and hat on. Albert crept in, making no sounds at all. First he took the red hat. The werewolf moved and made a noise. Albert's heart jumped. He told what happened next with sweat on his face in the club:

'I saw that there was a scar under its right eye – a scar caused by him being cut by a saw years ago, and I felt for the poor lad … he was a strange one at the best of times. Yet I knew I had to go on, and I managed to grab hold of the old shirt, being right careful to slip it over the big ears and the massive jaws and teeth. I thought he was waking up. My God, my heart was in my mouth … I mean, this ruddy great thing rolling over could wake up at any time, and then what would have happened to your old Albert?'

He took a swig of his pint and paused for a second. Just remembering all this was unsettling.

'My heart jumped again. Then I had to take his trousers off. Now, as a square-shaped, middle-of-the-road Tyke feller, I have no real experience in taking off men's trousers, except for my own, so I was out of my depth, do you follow? The hole in the trousers got bigger as I pulled the cloth tight … When I pulled it under his arse he moved as if he was waking up. But I had to keep tugging the trousers down, over the doggy knees and the doggy feet.'

Albert finished his pint and called for another. The landlord was only too happy to keep him supplied. The audience were spell-bound.

'Now I had all the clothes and I ran off to burn them. I got to a place where I thought I could burn them and be safe. It was an old garage in town. I started burning the hat first, but as soon as there was a wisp of smoke I heard the bloody howling of this lobhound thing ... and the sound of its *pad pad* coming closer and closer.'

'Go on Albert, go on!' someone said.

'So I took the clothes and ran to another place. This was a cave – deep in the darkness of that hill – you know the one at Forley where there's caves? It was deadly silent and dark when I lit a match, feeling sure that the damned thing wouldn't smell the stink of my fear in there. I started burning the trousers but as soon as there was a wisp of smoke I heard the howling again and then the *pad pad* of the dog's feet, coming nearer and nearer.'

'For Christ's sake, Albert, what did you do?' someone asked.

'I decided to run into town again, still clutching the clothes, trying to think of somewhere safe. Then I came close to the bank – you know – the one on Martin Square, and I remembered the vault where all the family savings were kept. Yes, that would be the right place, I thought. I went to the clerk and he checked who I was and asked to see proof of who I was and that ... then he gave me a key and a ticket number, and I locked myself in a giant safe, a strong-room, with a huge wheel you had to turn to seal the room. I started burning the clothes and I coughed and choked. It was a rotten place to die, I thought, choked like that, in a metal box! The clothes burned to a cinder, just a heap of black ashes. There was no sound of howling or padding of doggy feet. But as I finally came out again a fire alarm was ringing. I could hardly breathe lads ... I must have collapsed.'

We were all told, later, when things were back to normal, what happened after that. The next day, as Marisa lay in a hospital bed soon to have her baby, the nurse told her she had a visitor. It was her neighbour, Deano, and you know the strange thing? He was wearing the red hat and dirty shirt, and the trousers with holes in them, same as always.

Uncle Albert and the Job Application

FOLK AT GAWPHAM had long come to accept that Uncle Albert Peddle would never change, never move, never shift himself to do anything but live on scraps and bets and dreams. Nobody in his family would ever have imagined that he would walk into a room one day and announce to the world in general that he intended to apply for a job.

A job would have meant discipline, and he had none of that; a job would have meant getting out of bed by seven, and he couldn't do that; a job would mean looking smart and having some grooming, and he would not tolerate that. Therefore, his son and daughter-in-law accepted that what they had next door, through a thin wall and a door, was a man so set in his ways that you could wind him up and point him in a set direction, and he would go like a little tin soldier from point A to point B.

But then, in the midst of winter when he should have known better, Uncle Albert came downstairs after a long beer-induced sleep and said, 'I'm going to apply for a job.'

He was met with baffled stares, followed by questions about the need to have a bath, buy new clothes and dispense with his beloved flat cap. Most of all, Alice wanted to know what the job was. But there was no answer: only a mystery, and Albert's obvious delight in creating that mystery.

For that day and the day after, folk around the village noted that Albert Peddle was doing peculiar things. For a start, he was to be seen with pen and paper, even in the club, where he sat in his own chair, but shut off from all conversation so he could concentrate on the work in hand. Norrie Hissop led the general clamour to know what Albert was writing. 'Come on then, what's the big secret old lad? Have tha taken up writing poems?'

'Nay, it's his will … he's deciding who to leave all his worldly goods to, and it will not be thee, Norrie!' Tiny Sidebottom joked. But word spread, because Albert put his podgy hand around the sheet of paper so that nobody could peep at it, that it was indeed his will.

'But he's got nowt to leave … only maybe his dog and his beasts', Norrie said.

'I don't know, that allotment … there's a good acre of Yorkshire there, and four pigs and a dozen hens maybe. It all adds up!' Tiny chipped in.

Albert kept his secret: he went to great lengths to squat himself away in quiet spots so he could write. But he was struggling. Time and again, there would be bits of paper floating around the village with his distinctive scrawl on , saying 'Dear Sirs, I wish to apply' or sometimes it would be 'Dear Secretary, I am keen to be considered for … ' But these fragments only served to preserve the mystery.

Alice cornered him, though, after tea, before he could steal off to the club, and faced him with the question. 'Now Dad, I don't care what you're up to, but if you're going to be interviewed, new clothes are needed. Give us a few quid and I'll go buy them for you, love.'

He gave her a frown, but he saw the point. 'It'll mean breaking into my box!' He said, with a look of outrage on his face. 'But so be it … this is a very high position … it's a national responsibility, lass!' With that he went upstairs, and there was a rumbling noise, followed by a scraping noise, followed by a sound of some kind of tool being used, and then he came downstairs again with two five-pound notes in his hand. 'Will this buy me a new suit?'

'Depends where I buy it! But shoes as well … we'll see.'

Alice was delighted to be doing something to help. She was always left out of any of his plans, as was everyone else. The next day she went shopping in Forley and she was determined to buy something that would transform Albert into a smart, respectable older man.

Unfortunately, the rest of Gawpham thought the opposite. On the third day of his sitting in the club with pen and paper, they started to have some fun. Tiny Sidebottom opened the batting with, 'Na then Albert … tha does realise that tha's sixty-six years old? I mean, folk retire at that age, not apply for jobs, old lad!'

In the middle of the general laughter, Albert gave a scowl. 'Doesn't matter a bit … there's no age limit for this job, pal!'

'Well whatever the work, Albert, tha's an old bloke … see thy knees? They creak a bit. Then there's thy head – tha goes dizzy just walking to the bar!'

Albert ignored them all, just snapping back, 'Never mind all that – how does thee spell "efficient"?'

That night, he came home to the new clothes spread out on the table. Alice stood by with a smile. There was a dark grey suit, a pair of black shoes, a white shirt, and a tie with dark blue ripples in it. 'Right … you need a bath and a hair-wash, and then put these on so we can have a look at the new man', Alice said, holding the jacket up to his chest.

There was the sound of singing upstairs. Then followed stamping, banging and cursing, and finally Albert clomped downstairs and stood in the sitting-room, barely recognisable.

'By heck, Dad … it's magical!'

Even his son, Derek, normally quiet as a mouse, gave a cry of astonishment. 'Is that you Dad?'

'I didn't know myself, when I looked in t' mirror!'

Derek thought it was the right moment to ask that nagging question. 'Dad, what job is it? Can you reveal the truth?'

'I'll tell thee when I've finished the ruddy letter!'

The mystery went on. The next day he made it clear at breakfast that the letter had to be posted by twelve. Back in his usual clothes, he sat in the corner of the club, scribbling, having taken his seat long before his mates arrived. When Norrie and Tiny traipsed in for the eleven o'clock pint, when they all studied the racing pages, there was Albert, with dozens of scraps of paper scattered across the table, and even more bits littering the floor.

Albert sat with a satisfied smile on his face. 'Na then, get settled with thy pints … I've done the damned application at last, and I'm going to read it to thee for comments, afore it goes in the post.'

They all looked at him, and then at each other, and they were speechless for a few seconds.

'Does tha want me to check the spelling and the grammar, Albert, as I'm a professional historian?' Norrie asked, looking smug. All he had in return was a black look. Albert then readied himself, holding the sheet of paper up to the light, and adopting the stance of a vicar about to read a sermon from the lectern, and he read aloud:

Dear Sirs,

I have read in the paper as how the present public hangman is to retire. It is plain to me that the demands of such a terrible nasty perfession teks a lot out of a bloke, and it teks a special sort of ex-soldier to have the guts to yank a murdering sod into hell. I am that feller. All my life I have been killing things, like ducks and rats and such, an so I am applying for the vacancy before any other chap gets his neb in. I have very strong views on killers and rapists, as how they have no right to live and I would strangle them myself given the chance. For instance, that horrible beast who stabbed his missis last year in Forley – he's still breathing the air in Armley Jail. Instead, he should be feeding daisies. If you are interested, I could demonstrate my skill by showing thee how to snap a rat's neck in three seconds.

Yours faithfully,

Mr Albert Peddle

Ex-King's Own Yorkshire Light Infantry

There was a stunned silence. George Backhouse had joined the group, arriving in the middle of the letter-reading, and the landlord had walked over as well. As Albert put the paper down and gave a slight smile of satisfaction, the silence went on, until Norrie said, 'Tha can't be serious Albert? Tha can't send that, old lad! It's disgusting!'

They all chimed in with the same condemnation. Albert's confidence had been a warm, heartening feeling running through him, but now it froze into a chill.

'Wait till your Derek and Alice hear about this!' Tiny Sidebottom said.

'Well,' Albert gasped indignantly, 'I never thought my best pals would condemn a man for having a bit of ambition!'

'Ambition!' George put in, 'By hell Albert, stick to backing losers … tha's too old any road, to be killing folk!'

'Somebody has to do it!' Albert shrugged and took a pull of his pint.

'Aye … blokes who are a bit sick in the head!' Norrie joined in.

Word soon spread that Uncle Albert's job application was outrageous. He tried to keep it from Derek and Alice, but inevitably, they found out. When he finally staggered home, tipsy after a long session at the club trying to forget his embarrassment, he did what he usually did when he knew he was in disgrace. He opened the door, flung his cap into the room and shouted, 'Here's me hat … if tha' don't want me, chuck it back!'

Alice took pity on him and told him to come in. There was a long silence as he sat at the table and mumbled something about 'A daft idea any road.'

'Aye, we'll say no more … but at least you've got some lovely new clothes, Dad!' Alice said.

'Oh no … . take 'em back our lass, take 'em back!'

Derek and Alice shook their heads, and Alice then made her confession. 'Dad, I knew all the time. I'm not that daft you know. I clean your room … I saw that book with the horrible pictures of executioners … '

'Aye, and that sack of grain dangling from the hen-house rafters, that was a give-away. Tha were testing weights and ropes. We put two and two together', Derek said, 'And we decided that it was the best chance we'd ever have of getting you a new set of clothes!'

Uncle Albert the Wise Man

IN THE FIFTIES, when the war still cast its shadow over everybody's lives, reliable wisdom was hard to come by. Folk in Gawpham looked to the older generation to supply advice and knowledge. After all, they had lived through two world wars, and had been tested to the extreme. The men and women with wrinkles were considered to be worth consulting, unless they were complete drunks like Walter 'Speckled' Funnel, whose face was blotched through the effects of booze, or like Daft Ben whose advanced age had not brought common sense (he got lost on the way to the shops). Uncle Albert was, to many, one of these elders who had a certain *gravitas*, as Norrie Hissop would have said.

His corner in the club was often the scene of a consultation on matters of health, future prospects, romance and general advice about survival in a world only just free of ration books. Albert could say useful things about how to save money, how to avoid falling out with neighbours, how to cope with the Slacks when they destroyed your garden, how to find the winner of the Grand National, and so on. But his special expertise was in medicine.

Albert had a remedy for everything, or so he claimed. What was even more impressive was his skill in matters relating to the human body which would have been shameful and stressing if they had been discussed with a doctor. Hence old chaps came to him with spots on their lower parts; mothers brought babies with red patches on white faces; injured footballers came with lumps and bumps. He was afraid of nothing and he put this down to his treatment of wounds in the trenches when he had to act sharpish to save lives. 'Oh aye, young Jimmy Batty would have been a goner if I hadn't applied a tourniquet to his big finger.'

Then one day, as he sat in his corner studying the form, his worst client walked in. It was Mrs Nellie Slack and she had young Wilf with her. Wilf was a regular patient, having been a sickly child from his birth, and now there he was, five years old and looking white, ailing and fragile, holding his mother's hand and whining 'I don't want to see Mad Albert!' He screamed this over and over again as mother and child advanced across the saloon bar.

'What's the matter this time, Nellie?' Albert asked, expecting the worst.

'It's Wilfred … he can't go.'

'Well give him a push. They have to go to school, lass!'

'No, I mean he can't *go* … '

Albert looked the lad up and down. 'What does he eat?'

Nellie Slack ran through the Slack diet: porridge, bread and jam, and soup most of the time. 'And anything else they can pinch from Dora's corner shop!' Nellie added, folding her arms and frowning. 'What are you going to do? He's grunted and strained and he's not been for four days. He going to burst, Mr Peddle. *Do* they burst?'

'Nellie, take him home and I'll be there in ten minutes. Meet me by the midden.'

When he arrived, Nellie was there, and poor little Wilf was screwing up his face in pain. Nellie held out her hand and showed Albert something. 'See this … this is the last one he did … see the colour?'

There, nestling on her chubby palm, was a meagre mini-sausage of poo, and it was light grey.

Albert scratched his head. 'I can't grasp this … it's bloody dogs what have grey shit!' he said.

Desperate remedies were tried. After all, this horror was happening to a lad who had the full dose of reasonable food every day, and some concentrated orange-juice which he would have at school, *and* a number of stolen buns too. The outcome was a long session, sitting in the shared outside toilets, by the haunted midden behind Albert's cottage, having soap rubbed around his rectum by Uncle Albert, a man with his own secular version of Muscular Christianity. It involved a basin of water and Pear's soap. Young Wilf could never look at that Millais painting of Bubbles ever again without a throbbing sensation in his innards.

Some today might call that child abuse. In the fifties it was homely medicine, just like the poultices. Albert had most varieties of poultice, some even involving mushrooms, I recall. Some amateur medico in the Peddles' history was keen to experiment with these squares of linen packed with anything hot and strapped around the chest until you hopped around, being told that 'big boys don't cry' and the skills were handed down. Here was Uncle Albert, expert in all varieties.

'Mr Peddle, this lad has had every ailment except the Pudsey Palsy and had been warned against King Cough every time he sits bare-arsed on a flagstone.' Nellie said as Albert rubbed the soap around the child's bottom-end.

This was the time, I have since learned, when a whole generation had suffered the ravages of diphtheria and TB, and there was a feeling of revenge in the air against all unannounced bugs arriving in the village. Constipation was unusual, but Albert was prepared for anything. At last, after half an hour, there was a grunt and a plop. Wilf sat down on the floor, roaring his eyes red, and Nellie Slack gave Albert a kiss.

He earned his pints that night, and in fact Mr Slack came especially to buy Uncle Albert a few drinks. His reputation soared after that, and he was ready for anything. He had to be, because a few weeks later, as Albert sat in his corner, in came Nellie Slack, with Wilfred holding her hand, and he was whining again. Nellie started her long patter about her odd son.

'He's accident-prone, our Wilf, I know that of course: he's put his hand in the coal fire to grab a pencil, and he's stuck a darning-needle in his knee; he's put his fingers under the treadle of my sewing-machine, and he's fallen over the door-rod, splitting his head open. But until you got him shitting again he never had a crick in his neck!'

Albert, looking up from the racing paper, was looking forward to a nice, normal day until Nellie walked in. He repeated her words, 'Crick in his neck?'

'Show him, Wilf', she ordered, and the lad walked forward, quickly looked from side to side, and there was a snap of bones rammed together, just like when two sticks were rattled. 'That's a crick all right!' Albert said, perplexed.

'Well what are tha going to do? I mean there was no crick till you went down the midden with him!' She adopted that pose which everyone in Gawpham knew when she wanted trouble: arms folded, head slightly angled down on her chest, and her body swaying a little from side to side.

Albert decided to bluff his way out of it. 'Now lass, cricks is very rare, but the fact is that little childer grow out of 'em. Just be patient.'

'Beggar being patient. I want it put right!'

Albert was playing for time. All he could do was offer one of his placebos to keep her quiet. Back home he had a cupboard full of medicines, and in particular, he had his Trench Curative, known by the older residents of the village as 'gut rot'. It had been advertised back in the time of the Great War as *Mrs Applewick's Restorative* and the makers claimed that it cured everything from palsy to piles. In the trenches, it sent men to sleep, very deeply, and the chances were that when they woke up, their aches and pains would have gone. Albert had guessed at the ingredients, and in fact most of them were there in the smell from the bottle-neck, and he had made his own from nettle-juice, fruit and flower extracts ever since the war.

'Steady on Nellie … I've got just the thing! I'll bring a bottle round to you tonight after tea, and that'll put him right!'

'It had better, or I shall go to the bobby!'

This restorative was like nothing else on earth. It was a dull yellow colour and bubbled a little when stirred. Albert made up a new bottle, and added sugar as well, so the lad would drink it. Then Nellie came, and took the bottle, with a suspicious, guarded look on her face. 'It had better work, Albert Peddle!'

That night, after dashing his head from side to side again, just to make sure that the crick was still clicking away like a metronome, young Wilf and Nellie, along with all the other Slacks, were content that there was still an embarrassing problem. Wilf was given two tablespoons of the stuff and he lay there, waiting for the crick to disappear. Instead, he slept. By ten, he was deeply asleep and snoring as loud as his granddad who had only one lung.

The next morning, he was still fast asleep, and when Nellie shook him, he didn't move. There was a gut-wrenching scream from Nellie – so loud it was heard across three streets. One or two folk went out into the street and looked around. Then there was another scream. Shortly after that, Mr Slack came sprinting down High Fold, turned into the club and hammered on the door. In the club there was a phone, and he wanted an ambulance. 'Get the doctor – our Wilf's dead! he shouted. Someone heard, and then they told someone else, and they told someone else, and then someone told Alice and Derek as they sat at breakfast.

Now, Albert was out with Timmy, hunting rabbits. He was entirely ignorant of what was going on. By the time he reached home, he saw a crowd around the back of the cottage, outside the Slacks' place, and there was an ambulance. A doctor was giving Mrs Slack a telling-off. 'You've wasted precious time … we could have been at a real emergency, and instead you brought us out to see a boy who was – well, asleep!'

Nellie was about to go back inside when she caught sight of Albert, but he ran for cover, and hid out in the fields until opening-time that night.

There's no escaping your nemesis though, and at seven sharp, as Albert settled into his corner chair with a pint, in came Nellie Slack, with Wilfred. He was whining again. 'There you are … you old quack!' She was huffing and puffing like the Flying Scotsman, 'I thought you'd killed our Wilf … you and your restorer!'

'Well I'm very sorry ... but tha needs to know when a body's quick or dead, it seems to me!' His mates around the table found that amusing, and Nellie Slack stormed off with the cry of 'I'll never come for your help again, Albert Peddle ... and Wilf's still got the bloody crick!'

With a sigh of relief that he had lost his worst client, Albert sipped his pint. *Mrs Applewick's Restorative* had beaten the enemy again.

Uncle Albert and the Sow

A LBERT ALWAYS USED TO SAY, when the family got him talking about his early years, that his first memory was of falling under a sow. 'The second memory was seeing my mother in her coffin, there in the corner of the house, where we're sitting now!' he would say to Derek and Alice, as they sat around after tea and the winter cold closed in. That's when folk could really spur him on to tell his tales of the old days, when there was fog and mist outside, and a warm wood-fire banked up in the cottage.

This particular night, Alice had invited Tiny Sidebottom, George Backhouse and Norrie Hissop, and Uncle Albert was absolutely in his element. He loved nothing more than an audience and a place to sit where there was no escape for the listeners – unless they wanted to freeze outside in the Yorkshire winter.

'Oh aye,' he would say, 'all my life, since I was two feet high, I've been among beasts. I've looked after cows, hens, pigs, hosses, goats and dogs of course … can't forget dogs.'

As he made the last point, he would tickle Timmy, his golden Labrador, under one ear. 'But the biggest challenge I ever had in handling beasts was that sow. She was a monster, she was – she'd eat owt. She'd have thy hand off and swallow thy fingers in half a minute. I always wore leather gloves when I went to feed Poppy ... that was her name. She was a beautiful gert swine with a temper bad as that giant in *Jack and the Beanstalk*.

'My dad was a big, broad man but he went to see Poppy with a shiver of apprehension in him. It all came to a head one day when the sow was poorly. The difficulty with Poppy was that she didn't like humans. No, she had seen the worst of 'em when young, they reckoned. After that childhood marked by pain and suffering, she wanted to inflict the same on anybody what stank of human flesh. You see?'

It was one of those nights when Alice would make them all cocoa and there would be scones in the oven, and outside it could snow for all they cared – it could pack in and rise ten feet over the door for all the family cared when Uncle Albert warmed to his tale. That particular night, he spread out his thick legs and kicked off his old dusty boots, and went on.

'Now, sithee ... pigs will get any one of a thousand ailments. I remember once some college type sending us a survey here. He sent this form with boxes in it, trying to find out what sort of sickness our pigs was open to. Well, it listed dozens of these illnesses, some with long names, like. In the end I just put *Heft*. Is tha familiar with that our Derek?'

'Heft? No, I can't say I am.'

'"Has every f****** thing", that's what it means. I won't say the word in front of thee, Alice!'

Then it was on with his tale. 'Now, pigs get big bad ailments, like the shivers and the spews ... and they get little annoying ones like the scutters and the dizzies. These are not technical terms I know, but they describe the things. Now, Poppy had her own form of fever. She started dancing around, like she was in a fit, and chewed everything what came within three feet of her gob. We all watched her, the vet included, as he'd come especially to look at her, and my dad said there was only one thing for it. The old sow, she'd have to have an injection. See, the problem was that Mr Davison, the vet, he should have retired years back. His arms were like twigs and there was a certain shakiness to them, which was, as we know now, Parkinson's Disease. Back then, folk didn't retire: they just waited to drop dead.'

'What happened then, Dad?' Alice asked, intrigued.

'They all looked at me, and Mr Davison held out the syringe, wobbling in his shaky hand. "Go on lad ... you need bloodin' .... Never seen you stick a needle in a sow. First time for everything lad."'

'I didn't think I needed blooding, thank you. But the last thing I wanted was to seem like a coward. I took the needle – it was the size of a big chisel – and I looked at Poppy. She looked back at me. This Poppy, she had an uncanny ability to look inside your head and gauge whether or not you meant her harm. I could tell when she'd sussed me out, because she made a noise like when a bloody great hoss treads on your foot, and then she stamped a bit in the straw and her snout went up and down. I thought, *she's going to chew me to death.*'

'Then what, Dad?' Alice was nervous, cuddling up to Derek now, on the big sofa.

'Well, I thought, for a job like this I need armour. I wasn't going to let this gert big angry sow chew my hand off. The vet tried to comfort me. He said, "Don't worry Albert ... she likes you. I can tell." I thought, the lying git, he'll have me dead and laugh. It'll be something for him to tell at his posh vet's dinners. No, I got kitted out in layers. They all watched as I put three overalls on, then two pairs of gloves, and I wrapped a scarf around my right arm. Then I put a thick leather belt around my neck, like … to protect my neck in case she came at me and pierced an artery – and in I went – I slung a leg over the wooden fence and there I was. Well, I felt like a bloody matador, except I had a needle rather than a sword and cape. But I had a board as well. Tha knows, how we move pigs around with boards … well, I had a board. It's the one we use when we play snakes and ladders.'

'What? That board … it's been near pigs?' Derek asked, pulling a face.

'Aye … haven't you smelled the stink on it?' Albert stopped and took a drink of his beer. 'Now, I took a few careful steps towards Poppy. She backed off and snorted. In my mind, I ran through the options. Do I rush at her and dive at her, get the needle in her rump? Or do I coax her, gently sooth her and keep her distracted while I stick the needle in?'

'Mr Davison made up my mind for me, with the worst advice I ever had in my life – and that includes the order to go over the top at the Somme. He said, "She's female, lad, treat her like your girlfriend."'

'Well, I thought, what do I say to Christine Sidebottom? I usually said how nice she looked, so there we go … I have a plan. I crept forward, the needle behind my back, and I whispered, 'Na then you lovely bit o' pig flesh … tha's looking grand tonight … is that a new frock tha has on like? It suits thee … '

'What did the pig do, Dad?' Alice was so involved she was nibbling at her nails now.

'I decided, as I was near enough, I'd stick out a hand and grab her ear, then swirl her head round, and then dart my other hand round to stick the needle in. Unfortunately, Poppy had decided to go for me. She lunged and knocked me over. There was a thump as I hit the brick part of the sty, and then I felt something stab my backside and I was out cold. The last thing I remembered was seeing Poppy's gert big snout rubbing on my ear.'

'Were you badly hurt? What was in the syringe?' Alice asked, flushed with excitement.

'Oh, knock-out juice, along with some medicine to treat swine scutters. But when I came around, Mr Davison said, "Well done lad ... she didn't do any harm ... in fact I think she kissed you, lad."'

'Kissed me? A sow?'

'"Aye, she liked being soft-talked. Do you do well seducing women then, lad? Tha seems to have the patter." I could have clobbered him. I thought, he's the vet, he's the professional. Why couldn't he go in there and stab the creature? But after that, I'd been so scared, nothing ever frightened me again. In fact, there's a strange end to the tale. Tha sees, Poppy had a litter not long after, and tha knows what? Well, don't think I'm daft, but I think she brought 'em to show me ... she brought 'em to see the stupid little bloke who tried to stick a needle in her.'

'Thank God it was only that ... I thought you were going to say they all looked like you Dad!' Derek said, slapping his thigh and sending a ripple of laughter through the room.

Uncle Albert and the Hen-House

THERE WERE SOME PLACES around the village of Gawpham that had bad reputations: this was not for any reason connected with criminals or dangerous travellers; it was down to the presence, often alleged, of beings from the next world. The worst places for this were not mansions or hotels; they were not old moated granges or deserted asylums. No, the worst dark, unsettling locations were ordinary, workaday rooms or buildings, like, for instance, the old hen-house that features in one of Albert's family stories.

It was one of those times when Albert decided to come clean about his famous other-worldly experiences. Every now and then he liked to take some time away from his plans and machinations, his schemes for making money, and allow everyone to share a journey into the past with him. As he reached his late sixties, this nostalgic habit seemed to pop up more regularly, and folk relished it when he was in the mood for raking up something from his past. He always told these tales in a low, unsettling tone of voice, one he said he practised in the trenches, when he and his mates, with Death stalking all around them looking for victims, enjoyed a tin of weak tea and a cold pie in between attacks from the Bosch.

The gaggle of mates in the club were in the mood for one of Albert's tales and they pressed him to tell. He sat back, and said that he had a memory of the old hen-house from years back. 'You know what,' he said, 'going into a dark hen-house – it's ruddy terrifying – and this time, there was something from the other world in there. It were when me dad had died, and left it all to me … '

'What do you mean, Albert?'

He warmed to his story then.

'Well this day, I fed Monty, my old dog I had before Timmy, and he ravaged the food, such was his hunger. I sat back, still thinking whether or not to do any last jobs before night. There was still time, before dark, to take a look around outside. The night was closing in and I went out through a big, solid five-bar gate into a broad yard across a mixture of pebbles, hen droppings and horse manure. I heard the squeals and grunts of the pigs. When my dad had first bought 'em a month earlier, he'd christened them Doug and Dolly. According to the old man who had run the farm before retiring to the Dales, no piglets were on the way as yet.

'I remember looking across at the row of hen-houses and another gert big barn, which was used for any old stuff. The old man, my dad, had been open to any business that came his way, including removals and deliveries, and I remembered an ancient black van being in the barn, along with a row of rusty old bikes.'

'This was when tha were just taking over the farm then, Albert?' Norrie asked.

'Aye, it was strange, empty like … just me at the time. There was only a little strip of sunlight now, and scudding clouds, grey and threatening some rain. Further off, there was a dairy farm I remember – it belonged to old Coppard – and then a row of poplar trees and the little wilderness of the Drang Woods. The past came back in snatches as I walked to the barn: memories of playing outside the school up the road, and then the shouts of the boys on the high wall of the club.

'It was too dark really, to do much. I reached the barn and pushed the big door. I hadn't locked it earlier, typical of me, lads! If there was a light of any kind, I had no idea where the switch was, so I stood with the door open behind me, only just able to make out a straw-covered space where the old van and the bikes had been. Looks like I have a clean white canvas then … open spaces and empty rooms, all for me, I thought, looking around. The breeze behind was stirring some loose sacks, piled by a heap of old wooden boxes, and I felt a bit anxious though I didn't know why.'

'Then what Albert? For God's sake man, get on with it!' said Tiny Sidebottom.

'Right, well, there was a faint rustle in the straw and for a second I caught a glimpse of a small, dark shape darting across and into the workshop, where I could just make out the forge. The old man had been a blacksmith, you remember?

'Hmm … rats. Of course. I smiled to myself. But I couldn't stave off the shiver I felt go through me, just thinking about having rats running around the place – I mean, it was my home now … our last farm, before we cut down to the allotment like.

'Any road, then it was time to get ready and walk down to the club, show my sociable side. But, walking back to the house in the dark now, I caught sight of a building I'd forgotten to check, the hen-house; there was a window with curtains and a very dim light inside. I stopped, and looked closely. The wind was stronger now and loose planks were flapping on the old buildings around me. I screwed up my eyes to focus on the shed, and I just sensed a blur of movement, as if somebody had moved past the window, there was someone inside. But there was no one else there – or at least, there shouldn't have been, unless Dad had had some kind of guest and not told me. Or, well, what else could it have been?'

'Your dad ... the ghost of your dad, Albert!' George said, as if it was all so simple.

'Funny you should say that, George ... because the next morning, in the cold light of day, I'd been out to collect some eggs, and as I walked back, I thought I saw, through the window in the kitchen, my Dad sitting there, waiting for his morning tea, just like he always did, and when I opened the door, I heard his voice say, in a whisper, "There's more than hens in there lad."'

It was his best tale, that one, never to be topped.

Uncle Albert and a Last Goodbye

UNCLE ALBERT WAS NOT ALWAYS A CLOWN, though some said he was a natural one and should have had cap and bells like the old jesters. He was good with a jest, but there was another side to him, and this story concerns the Albert without his joker's outfit. In fact, I've heard it said that he never meant anything he said and he stretched everything like he was always talking with his words on tiptoe, but the village folk will never forget the night he spoke about the war – the one nearly everybody knew back in the day, when bomb-sites were well remembered and people still bothered to keep their ration books.

Usually, you couldn't get any peace out of Albert once he got settled in that corner seat in the club. His day was done, and his face set, intent on entertaining rather than being entertained. The stories were waiting to spill out of him, and all it needed was a question to set him off with a good tale. But there were some rare nights when he was in one of his 'Wordsworth moods' as Norrie called them. He was asked

what he meant by that and Norrie said, 'Well, poetry like …
Albert has a grand poet in him.'

The general opinion was that the poet in Albert specialised
in mucky limericks but he was known to have a go at an ode
or two. Anyway, on one night in particular – the whole crowd
at the club remembers it – as soon as we sat down he started.
Pints were being supped and coughs coughed, and before
anybody else spoke, Albert said, as if to nobody in particular,
'It started off in confusion that day … I should have known it
were fated to be black.'

'What day Albert?' Norrie asked.

'The third of February, 1941. I shall never forget. See, tha
knows nowadays I'm famous for being a rational man … a
man in control? Well … ' He paused to allow the chuckles to
subside as folk responded to his last remark. Then he carried
on regardless. 'Well, back in the war, I was different. I always
seemed to be in bother, trying to do too many things at once.
I was the sort of bloke what sends a betting-slip to the taxman
and a tax return to t' bookies! That's how the black day started,
with one of my muddles.'

'Go on then', Norrie pressed him, intrigued.

'Well, I was queuing in Harry Clegg's fish shop … I think
all he had was tiddlers like, but we still queued, like daft
beggars. Any road, I stood there, with my tweed jacket on …
Bessie had washed it like. So there I was, frustrated as a dog
on a prairie, when I noticed folk looking at me. Then I ignored
'em and looked t' other way like, and then they still looked
at me. Then finally Harry said, "Albert, has tha seen thysen!"
Well, I was stumped by that. Then a voice behind in the queue
said, "Pegs, Albert … pegs!" I was still flummoxed, and then
someone reached over to me and took a peg off my shoulder.

Blow me, the pegs were still on the coat, from t' washing line like! I felt a right clouthead.'

'Well it was hardly a black day then Albert, surely?' someone asked. More folk were gathering now, some standing up, because Albert was clearly in an uncommon state of mind. Somebody whispered, 'Hey … he's on about t' war!'

Now, everybody in Gawpham knew that Albert had been an air-raid warden in the last war, and that he had fought in the first big 'un, but he didn't talk about it much.

'Now, that's how the day started. It was a day when Hitler had it in for Leeds. It was just before I jointed t' fire brigade, and I was still on air-raid duty. Oh yes, he knew where the ordnance factory was. His bombers were going for that … wanting to smash all the long black roofs that were harbouring tanks and cannon and God knows what else. So the bombers came. One time I was walking up a slope in Beeston, and as I got to t' top, there was this silver-grey bloody Hun plane, seeming to fly right towards me nostrils. But that weren't the black day … no, see, after giving up the queue for fish and going home, it were time for me shift. I put the air-raid warden coat and hat on, and got my whistle, and by four I were ready. Bessie was in the kitchen making soup out of brass farthings and axle-grease, and I asked about t' pegs.'

He stopped for a second and gathered his thoughts.

'She said she were right sorry that she left the pegs in, but said, "But tha's a daft ha'porth any road for not noticing the things were still in the shoulder! Honestly, what am I going to do with you!" Then tha knows what … she said something else. She squeezed my hand and she said, "You're my hero, Albert Peddle, you do know that?" I nodded and grunted, like blokes do.'

There was a tear welling up in his eyes, but he stopped, wiped it clear, and carried on.

'I gave her a kiss and she said she had some baking to do, and I'd better be off.'

Albert smiled, giving all his listeners a little share of whatever happy thoughts were now in his head.

'I should have seen then that she wasn't herself. But I'm about as thick as Scots porridge when it comes to noticing things. Any road, off I went, walking up and down the roads, shouting, 'Put that light out!' Darkness soon fell. There was snow on the ground and a real bite in the air, tha knows. Well, the confusion went on. There hadn't even been a siren yet, but some daft beggar bumped into a wall and I had to find a plaster for his head. Then some bairns came running out of Jaggers' shop with him after 'em, shouting "Stop thief!" Now I wasn't a bobby, but I grabbed one and took him back, turned him upside down and out came some boiled sweets the size of golf-balls.'

He finished the dregs of his pint of bitter and wiped his mouth. 'The black day were gathering ...'

'Get him another pint, somebody!' a voice called from the back row of listeners.

The beer was put in front of him and he looked around, then carried on. 'See, folk today, they read about the fear of being in a war, but they don't know it ... deep down. When some barbarians are up there, dropping bombs on your homes and your bairns, well, it's ... well, it fills your days with nerves, so that you walk around feeling there's a few bricks piled on your chest ... it were like that on that night when I got to Cartman Street. It was when the sirens started.'

We had a short explanation of the ordnance factory then. He told us it had been where they made munitions in the first war. 'Aye, Bessie had been a canary lass ... they got yellow in their hair and on their coats, making shells for us Tommies right? Well, now Adolf had his sights on the place.'

Albert paused to check he wasn't boring anyone. 'I'm an old bloke going on about t' war ... say if you're browned off with it.'

Folk nodded and made encouraging sounds, so he took up his tale again. 'Well, Cartman Street yes ... not too far off the ordnance factory ... folk were running to the shelters. I shouted at one or two, and they told me to shut up, like they always did. Then, it seemed like twenty minutes after t' siren like, the drone of the engines came over us. My heart shivered in me chest, I'll tell tha! Up there they were, in that dark sky, and t' snow came heavier then ... there was just the engines, and then this whine as the bombs started ... and I were still walking round, tapping on lighted windows. Then, well, I looked towards home and where my own house stood, and I whispered to the Almighty to save me and mine ...'

There was complete silence in that corner of the club as he paused again and sipped his beer. Some of his listeners, his close friends, knew what was coming, but others didn't. Albert's war with Hitler was not well known.

'Right, now time went on, and the bombs and the sirens were coming, and I had a coating of snow on my coat and over my moustache, as I had a military one then, still there from t' first war when we all had 'em .... and I got to a point where I just sat on a doorstep, choosing one with a nice cover over t' doorway, a posh place, and I waited for the heathens to bugger off home to Hunland. But, what I want to tell tha is ... see, I heard her voice, coming across the valley there, from Gawpham right over to Beeston, and it were like a whisper ... and she said, "All is well in the best of all possible worlds."'

'Then what did you do Albert?' someone asked.

'What did I do? I don't know to this day whether I'd fallen asleep on that doorstep or whether it really was her voice, but t' raid was over and I was hopping it back home quicker than a whippet. It were a mile or so, that's all, and I had my bike. I'd left it on the street corner. I laughed at myself as I biked home, thinking how right my name was – Albert Peddle. I started wondering if all the Peddles back through history had been bikers. Happen there had been an Albert Peddle who rode a bike for King William the Conqueror. Then I thought, no, there were no bikes then surely. All that daft thinking was to distract my mind from the thought of bombs. Then I got back home, to the end of our street. We lived in a row of terraces back then, tha sees – it were Balaclava Street – maybe some of you remember? Three streets were hit ... all but three houses survived.' Someone saw the tears welling up and gave him a hanky.

'Did your house get hit Albert?' This was a young voice, someone new to Albert and his tales. He seemed to like that. He always needed an audience, but best of all he liked a new one.

'No lass, no. I started walking from the end of t' street. Every house I passed was half-wrecked. It was like a scene from Hell that met my eyes. Voices yelled out that a wall was falling or that something was about to blow or topple onto some poor beggar. There were firemen and bobbies everywhere. They all knew me. Some bloke shouted out, "You've been lucky Albert!" Well I wasn't. I got to our front door, you see, pushed it open, and walked through ... no damage anywhere ... everything was as it was when I'd left for my shift. Everything except one. Bessie was in her armchair, but Mrs Tempest and Mrs Medd were with her, standing by her. She said ... Mrs

Medd that is ... she said she was so sorry. "I think her heart gave way", she said to me, grabbing my arm and leading me to my Bessie.'

'"I came in to see if she was well, and I found her ... I thought at first she was asleep!" Mrs Tempest said, plucking at her pinny, fidgeting like we do when there are no words to be found except the stupid ones.'

Everything went silent again. The stillness seemed to spread from the corner across to the bar and to the next circle of seats and tables. Heads all turned to look at Uncle Albert. We wondered whether all his words had dried up.

'She were sitting back, her eyes now closed. "Bless her," the women said, "bless her, Albert, she was a grand lass to you." Then Mrs Tempest said, in a whisper, "Ee, I had to smile, Albert ... see!" She held up a shirt from the washing-basket, and there were two pegs, in the shoulders.'

Uncle Albert the Storyteller – and What Happened

THIS COLLECTION OF TALES has to end with a story told by Albert himself, to us kids. He was a talented storyteller, but he never read any books. He was told tales by his mother, he said, and she was part-gypsy. This was his favourite, a very old story from somewhere or other, and he told Derek and Roy and the rest of us to sit and listen and then ask a sensible question at the end.

On this occasion, he said that when he finished the tale, he wanted us to ask a question. 'Make it a sensible question, lads, to prove you've been thinking and that – listening properly.'

We nodded and promised, wanting him to get on with it, and Albert began …

Now this story is called Nail Soup and it's famous, but I'm telling thee it in my own way … There was a lad who had lost his parents. Both had died when the great lurgy came to the land. He was just ten years old and was all alone. That means he had no family, but he did have lots of servants, because his parents had been very rich and they left him plenty of money so that as long as he lived he would never have to worry about not being able to afford things.

His parents had called him Rex because that means 'king' in Latin. They wanted him to be a king of a kind – a king of wealth. They wanted him to live like a king, although his home was in the countryside in England. He lived in a massive house: a mansion with ten bedrooms, three bathrooms, a swimming pool, stables for hosses, a garage wide enough for three cars. He bought a Jaguar car that cost as much as most people's homes. He had servants to buy his clothes, cook his food and do all the jobs around the house.

But he had a problem: he didn't want or need any other folk. Folk thought he was having one big sulk. He didn't think this was a problem, but the servants knew it was. Every day was full of games and all kinds of toys. He never did bother to talk to any neighbours. He wasn't interested in friends, not even the ones you could meet at school, as he had a private tutor who came to the home and then went home, paid by the hour, like posh folk do.

His chief servant, Ozzy, always came to him every day after breakfast and asked him what he needed for that day.

'Rex just needs a new TV. He's bored with the one he has, Ozzy.'

'Any special kind of television, Sir?'

'The biggest you can get, Ozzy.'

Days passed with every kind of pleasure you could imagine. Except for his bedroom, all the rooms in the house were full of different amusements. One room had one-armed bandits; one had a train set with tunnels and mountains; one had indoor ten-pin bowling; one had a library of eight thousand story-books.

Outside there was a black stallion he rode once a year, when he showed off to the servants and the local kids. He made the servants film him on the horse and then tell him how brilliant he was, and how he was better than Lester Piggott.

Then one day he came downstairs and there was no breakfast ready for him. Rex actually had to walk through two rooms to look for Ozzy and the other servants. But there was nobody to be seen. He called out but there was no answer. Then he rang Ozzy to see if he was still at home, but there was no reply. Rex found some cereal – his favourite *ChoccyRiceyBlobs* and he put some toast in the toaster, after taking some time to work out how you toasted bread. He was muttering and complaining, 'Somebody will lose his job for this … I can get other servants … easy!'

Later that day, after reading one of his books he felt uneasy. The house was completely silent. No servants had arrived. Then, at six in the evening he had to think about food. He was sitting in his big armchair wondering what to do when the doorbell rang.

This was strange. He had no memory of ever opening the door to anyone. The servants always did that for him. But the bell rang again. He decided to get to his feet, walk through some more rooms, and look for the front door. He followed the sound, buzzzzz buzzzzz.

Then there was the door. It was huge and wooden. There was a shiny gold handle, so he pulled that down and yes, the door opened, creaking, making a noise like a sick frog. I'll have to get Ozzy to fix that, he thought.

Standing before him on the doorstep was a young boy about his age. He was scruffy. His clothes were torn and his hair looked a mess. He wore a heavy coat and carried a bag that seemed lumpy, it was so full of stuff.

'Morning mister. I just wondered if you had anything to eat. I haven't eaten a proper meal in days.'

'No way, you tramp!' shouted Rex, and shut the door in the boy's face.

Then he started walking back through the rooms, but he thought, okay, just a minute, maybe that boy could be a servant? He walked back and opened the door again. The boy was still walking towards the gate, which was a very long walk from the front door.

'Hey you, come back!' Rex called. The boy walked slowly back, smiling.

'You changed your mind, Sir?'

'Well, only if you can cook.'

'Sure I can. I'm a traveller. I can cook anything. I can make you nail soup.'

'What?' Rex actually smiled – which was a very rare thing for him to do. 'Nail soup? Don't be ridiculous, nobody eats nails. There's no such thing as nail soup!'

'There is, just show me the way to the kitchen', the boy said.

Rex had some trouble finding his way through the rooms and reaching the kitchen. It was the size of a department store.

'Wow, this will do nicely', said the lad. He took a pan from a rack and filled it with water. 'Now here's a nail, and I have a little bit of parsley in my pocket – didn't pinch it from your garden though Sir!'

He put the parsley in the pan of water with the nail.

'You wouldn't have any carrots or peas would you Sir? That would go well.'

Rex started looking around. He opened drawers and fridges and finally found some vegetables. One pack had a picture of peas on it and he recognised them. 'Ah, peas … these are

111

peas!' He gave some peas to the boy, and these were added to the water. So now they had peas, parsley and a nail.

'You know what would be great with these? Some onions. Would you happen to have any onions Sir?'

Rex looked around again and yes, there was a pack of red onions. It said 'onions' on the packet, so he knew they were onions. The boy asked Rex to peel and slice the onions but he didn't know how. Ozzy always did that. Rex just knew that sometimes he was served onions.

'Watch!' said the boy. He peeled the skin and sliced the onion. He then started weeping. Rex was worried. Why would the boy be crying? All he had done was peel an onion. He asked why he was upset. The boy explained that onions made you cry and he told Rex to put his nose near the onions. Then Rex felt his eyes go sore and he wept. After he started crying, it was so funny that he laughed.

The boy set the table. Usually Rex just had a tray with his food on, served to him while he sat in his favourite armchair and read a comic. But the boy put out placemats and cutlery. He put a jug of water in the middle of the table as well.

'Now Sir, if we had some gravy that would be wonderful. Do you have any?'

Rex was enjoying himself. He liked gravy, and again he looked on the shelves until he found a jar with 'gravy' written on it. The boy put some in the soup, and soon they sat down and the soup was served. It was delicious. Rex's face was just one big smile.

'It's really tasty ... do you like it?' asked the boy.

'Yes, but I can't taste the nail.' Rex frowned.

'Oh the nail ... that's the best ingredient. That adds something lovely, but you can't even taste it', said the boy.

Rex thought, and then he knew what he meant.

A short time later, Ozzy came in, saying he was sorry. 'Sir, I'm so late, the traffic was terrible … '

But Rex said, 'Don't worry Ozzy. I know I've been crying but I've had a great time … and guess what? I know where the front door is!'

Albert stopped and looked around, 'Any questions kids?'

'Aye,' asked Roy, 'Did they have puddin'?'

About the Author

Stephen Wade was born in Leeds and brought up first in Churwell, and then Whitkirk. As a child, he was a dialect speaker, and in his stories he recreates the village life he knew and the local life and talk he relishes as a writer. In his earlier book, *Passion for the Park* (2012) he wrote about Sunday football in Leeds in the sixties, and told his own story as a Leeds loiner. Stephen also worked as a writer in several prisons, and has written on this in *An Angle from Above* (2006) He is perhaps best known as a writer on the criminal history of his home county, and his book *Unsolved Yorkshire Murders* was a Waterstones book of the month. His other main works in this area are *Foul Deeds and Suspicious Deaths in Halifax* (2004) and *Heroes, Villains and Victims of Bradford* (2008). He is currently writing a comic novel about a Yorkshire entertainer, *Harry Mossop Makes it Big*.